ATOMS
NEVER
TOUCH

ATOMS
NEVER
TOUCH

micha cárdenas

AK PRESS

Praise for *Atoms Never Touch*:

"A shockingly powerful, wrenchingly beautiful queer cyberpunk fable from debut novelist and veteran artist micha cárdenas. In this slim yet unforgettably striking story, cárdenas shows us the world we live in through a dark mirror, transforming the language of cybernetics, quantum physics, and neurobiology into haunting metaphors for heartbreak, social struggle, and revolution. cárdenas fearlessly plumbs the depths of her characters' terror and trauma as they resist the depredations of fascism and digital surveillance, but also infuses her novel with hope, healing, and possibility."
—**Kai Cheng Thom, author of** *Fierce Femmes and Notorious Liars: A Dangerous Trans Girl's Confabulous Memoir*

"I see this book as in the lineage of Octavia Butler's *Kindred*, an explicitly quantum exploration of the possibility of ancestral love. I love the characters and the queer questions they raise with their living. And I love the message, which is that love is the code, love is the pass, love is the key, love is all, love is all, love is all." —**Alexis Pauline Gumbs, author of** *Undrowned*

"What more could we ask for? T4T love and sex, antigovernment sabotage, travel through the multiverse! *Atoms Never Touch* is nourishment for radicals surviving the current apocalypse." —**Dean Spade, author of** *Mutual Aid: Building Solidarity During this Crisis (and the Next)*

Atoms Never Touch
Emergent Strategy Series No. 10
© 2023 micha cárdenas
This edition © 2023 AK Press (Chico / Edinburgh)

ISBN: 9781849355285
E-ISBN: 9781849355292
Library of Congress Control Number: 2023935634

AK Press
370 Ryan Avenue #100
Chico, CA 95973
USA
www.akpress.org
akpress@akpress.org

AK Press
33 Tower St.
Edinburgh EH6 7BN
Scotland
www.akuk.com
akuk@akpress.org

Please contact us to request the latest AK Press distribution catalog, which features books, pamphlets, zines, and stylish apparel published and/or distributed by AK Press. Alternatively, visit our websites for the complete catalog, latest news, and secure ordering.

Cover design by Herb Thornby
Printed in the United States of America on acid-free paper

For May, and Isla, all my friends who carried me through, and all our hopes for a livable future.

FOREWORD

by adrienne maree brown

I remember the first time I experienced the mind of micha cárdenas.

She was keynoting the Allied Media Conference in Detroit several years ago, discussing a project that involved setting up water stations throughout the desert grounds of our southern border. This direct action supported the survival of migrants running towards life through militias and border control agents hunting them. In my memory, she wore a red dress and had red lips, and I thought, "This trans-Latina femme is the future."

A few years later, I talked with micha about another project she was working on—converting old tires into affordable bulletproof vests for communities targeted by police. Again, I was thrilled by how her mind worked, looking past the stuck places of our oppressed conditions, looking for solutions with the things that we have available to us.

Whether watching micha dance, perform, read poems, or innovate technology, I never fail to be expanded by the range of her imagination and how it is always rooted in her rigorous self-examination and willingness to grow and change to make more possible.

When I learned she was writing fiction, I knew that I was a future fan. *Atoms Never Touch*, the novel you hold in your hands, is beyond my wildest dreams—an original work of micha cárdenas fiction as part of the Emergent Strategy Series! A work of alternate universes and love between trans women, a remarkably tender story of abolition and antifascism, a work that satisfies and plants seeds for wanting more.

I'm so grateful micha trusted us with this novel. She is letting us see how many worlds coexist in any given moment; she is showing us how *we* are the portals to futures where we can be loved and held and trusted with the gifts of our own lives.

CHAPTER 1.

Cora sat on the toilet, gazing down at the beige-lined pattern of the floor tile as it flickered and slowly tilted, before reality snapped back into place. There it was again, that slow, spinning feeling. She had thought it was gone, but here it was again. Along with her eye twitch and her nightmares, here was another thing that had worsened after the election. These moments when it happened—this feeling—seemed also to accompany a slowing of time. She would be sitting there and suddenly notice that her visual field was slipping, turning ever so slightly. Then came the sinking in her stomach and the thought of, "Oh no, it's back." The doctors said it was "benign positional vertigo." She knew it was more. Vertigo didn't explain the flicker.

Sitting up and sighing, she felt the familiar pain in her neck that had also returned since the election. She looked at the inside of the stall door, gray and free of dialogue until she turned on her auglenses. One of her favorite things about women's restrooms, different from men's rooms, was that they were usually full of aug graffiti:

"You are beautiful, just ~~as you are~~

~~just lose a few pounds~~

~~no shit~~

just learn to see it!"

"Report him at <u>pussygrabsback.augspot.aug</u>!"

"FUCK EMOS DATE GOTHS"

"FUCK GOTHS DATE GIRLS"

"FUCK EVERYONE AND ENJOY IT"

were just a few of the philosophical debates in the layers of scribbled words that could be seen with the slight gesture of the head that enabled or disabled the optional content in her auglenses. The lenses used a simple algorithm to determine which gesture the user made based on changes in visual content, no longer relying on the accelerometers of earlier, clunkier devices.

She took a deep breath, centering herself before going back out into the world. Looking at the stall door, spacing out. She still missed Juana. She missed Juana's black curls, her voice, her tenacity. She could hear other people coming in and out of the restroom. She heard the automated announcement in the mechanical female voice, "Please report any suspicious persons to airport security. Any luggage left behind may be subject to inspection or destruction. Thank you for your cooperation. Together, we can make the Cascadia Airport safer."

These words always gave her pause, for so many years her appearance had been somewhere on the suspicious spectrum. Is gender transgression suspicious? Are the skin and hair of a Latina woman suspicious? Is a Latina woman covered in tattoos wearing fierce eyeliner suspicious? Why aren't people calling airport security all day to report, " I suspect that the older white woman in the seat across from me in the waiting area is planning violent actions against me because I'm not white and my gender doesn't fit into the realm of her understanding!" Of course, she knew what qualifies as suspicious, and that includes anyone Black, Muslim, queer, trans, and certainly anyone poor enough to lack the telltale red indicator dot in their retina, evidence of an active aug device.

She finally stood up. It was only a couple years ago that she had surgery, and when she went under to have her gender confirmed, she also got her auglenses. In the last few years, it had become more common for people getting any surgical procedures to have their auglenses implanted at the same time.

Leaving her stall, she went to the sink and washed her hands. She placed her backpack on the brushed aluminum counter next to the sink. It was not long ago that this was a moment of terror for her; before surgery, she would do this basic task as quickly as possible. In an airport, she had no idea who else might be in the bathroom. If they didn't see what they thought looked like a woman, they might stop her. They might call security. They might call the police. They might harass and detain her. She might not get where she was going. In those moments, she would focus only on her hands as she washed them, and she would never make eye contact. If no one really looked at her, they might not have the chance to evaluate where she fit. They might not use their aug to compare and analyze her or to look up her image on the networks.

Now she felt differently. She felt safer knowing that her surgery had given her the biological changes she had so deeply desired, and had also etched a series of small, nearly imperceptible changes to her face, neck, shoulders, and gluteus median structure that only the detailed algorithms of an aug might register. By understanding the facial analysis algorithms of augs, as well as the body and gate analysis algorithms, surgeons were able to shift the image seen by aug users to be undeniably female. It was one of many ways to interact with the pattern recognition algorithms that were a normal part of vision for so many people every day. There were other, more subversive uses of hacking aug algorithms as well that Cora had only read about.

She washed her hands and looked at herself in the mirror. She often even made eye contact with other women in the mirror, now. And she did so, allowing her aug to register all the details it does in such moments, calculating shared interests and match percentage based on the public elements of her dating profile alongside the other woman's sexual availability, preferred pronoun, travel destination, and in this case, only the first initial of someone who seems to care about her privacy.

But Cora wasn't interested in meeting new people. She looked at her reflection again and took a deep breath. She thought she looked tired. Her eyes were a bit red from crying, and dots of her mascara were below her eyes. She wiped them away. In the mirror, the remaining minutes and seconds until boarding time flashed transparently next to her face, so she would get to the plane on time. She had five minutes left, she saw as she leaned in close to wipe the mascara away. The proximity of the display to her face made her back away a bit, surprising her.

5:00 board Flight 305 to Bogotá

4:59 board Flight 305 to Bogotá

4:58 board Flight 305 to Bogotá

This display flashed in place. It wasn't slipping, and neither was anything else. Cora stood up straight, trying to see herself. Well, this would be a cliché moment in a television story about a trans woman, she thought, but it was real. Looking in the mirror was often complex for her. She grabbed her backpack with her laptop in it, the bootable USB drive with the malware, the scripts to deliver it, and all the tools she would need to get into the airplane's Wi-Fi connection without being tracked. She was not just going to let this new president put even more people in cages. For years, she'd been going to protests for prison abolition and against police brutality, but when she saw an article about the Law Enforcement Activity Portal, the LEAP, being used against striking students, she realized that it was the perfect target for an abolitionist hack. LEAP relied on a computer system with a public-facing interface allowing local, state, and federal law enforcement agencies to access a single database of criminal records. This setup was an invitation for a hacker, such as her, to break in and erase everything.

An airplane is a perfect place for a hack. Most internet connections are tied to specific geographic locations, so if you're detected, the feds might just come knocking on your door. But on an airplane, once you break into the Wi-Fi connection, you have a perfectly anonymous satellite internet connection with no geographic location. While there was always the risk of being trapped, Cora was confident that no one else on that airplane would have the technical know-how to distinguish a digital attacker from a passenger watching the latest trash movie on their auglenses.

The vulnerabilities were easy enough for Cora to find and exploit. The login for LEAP might've been the biggest challenge, but she simply looked up the recent, published exploits of the login system and found that the administrator had been too slow to update it. Once she was inside LEAP, her plan was simply to reverse engineer the database code that was accessed during searches. With some cross-site scripting, she could get server-side and see the database queries—the code that *requests* data— from federal and state criminal records databases. She simply had to change those queries to write statements—into code that *writes* data—to do some serious damage. Seriously, fucking child's play. She hoped that in this time of transition, with no records of arrest histories or convictions, a lot of people could finally be freed from their cages.

CHAPTER 2.

She held me so tenderly, one arm around my shoulders, fingers inside me, and as I shook, the molecules around us found new arrangements. The change in reality was subtle. After she was gone, I saw that some of the details in my large print of the Milky Way above my bed had changed. Only a few stars had moved, a few rocks had new ripples in their skin. The pale blue color of my clock's display was slightly different. The effects were quantum, changes in possibility maps of proton clouds, but as I fell asleep, I knew that I would never see Beatriz again.

Blurry ovals of blue light crossed with lines of shadow through them slowly moved back and forth in my vision as I awoke the next morning naked in bed, lying on my back looking at the ceiling. I wasn't ready to get up. I rolled to my side and enjoyed the moment of Astrud Gilberto's dreamy voice languidly swaying across the notes of bossa nova. I looked at my arm in front of me in bed, savoring the leftover memories of pleasure from the night before. I remembered her breathing my name into my ear as she held me, "Rea . . . "

The blankets and pillowcases were covered in a print of hand-drawn vines of garnet peonies, creating a warmth I was not ready to leave. As Astrud sang of "quiet nights of quiet stars, quiet chords from my guitar . . ." something in the notes moved something inside me. I thought of all those I've lost in other universes, and I wept. On my side, I brought my hands to my forehead and my knees closer to my chest, shoulders shaking from crying. The warm tears dropped off my face into my hands and darkened the sheet. So many loves lost, to universes I can never get back to.

The kettle cried later in the morning as I cooked my breakfast. The kettle cries so loud that I always run to turn it off because the downstairs neighbors must hear it. The music moved on to the sweeping beauty of Carla Morrison, the blinds open, winter blue sunlight lighting my apartment. The slow rising on the synthesizer pad stretching out many simultaneous high notes, lifting slowly, filling out a lush space, gradients of purple and pink, wavy lines, electric. As I fill the French press with ground coffee, the rich smell of the Colombian roast embracing my awareness.

The synth was punctuated with a slow dark beat, giving the space of sound a pulsation and rhythm that leaves trails within the field created by the synthesizer, like a heart filled with both sadness and grace. I was learning to find peace and serenity, and this moment was one of my favorites of the day. Sitting, I drank my second cup of coffee, looking out my window across the bay, the land on the other side showing through the mist, the winter light in rays.

Bianca and I met on Metatext, in an online group for queers in the city, a few weeks later. We chatted for the next couple hours while I watched a video stream with a friend on the couch. Browsing her photos on Metatext, I saw that she was attractive in a quiet way, which I now understand as a maternal way. Seeing photos of her holding her baby niece only made the fantasy gears in my heart turn faster. I wanted to be a mother.

Our first date was the weekend I arrived in the city. I came from work, didn't even have time to change out of my black jeans, just took off my work shirt to wear the camisole underneath it with my leather jacket. I parked in a hurry. I spotted her in the street, and we just began walking together without missing a beat, as if we had already known each other, as if our molecules had the right arrangements for bonding already. It was really the pattern of codependency that was so familiar, though I didn't know it yet.

She still held me at bay for weeks. One night we were making out on a park bench near her apartment, and I suggested we go to her place, but she didn't want to move too fast. If only I would have listened to her. But I couldn't. I was still living in my own reality. I hadn't really accepted the truth of my situation, the ways that my neurochemistry is different. The truth is that my brain doesn't work like other people's. I can see that now, now that I've dug into the parts of my memory that I was unable to see before, now that I've acknowledged the trauma I experienced when I was abused as a child. It was hard to see. Writing poetry, making films about my experience wasn't enough. Every time I moved into a new reality and shifted out of the previous one, it was as if the words in my writing and the films I made to document my life had also adjusted their molecules to match the new quantum reality.

It was so hard, then, to perceive the changes in front of my face because it was a complete reality, with its own logical completeness, but in a different quantum universe. I wish I knew what unique combination of cortisol, dopamine, serotonin, and oxytocin in my brain created the conditions to allow my atoms to touch those of another person. I'm sure there are people who would kill me to find out, so I can't ever let anyone know.

It was months later, months of drunken nights together, so many nights of worldmaking sex, so many early dawns where we realized with gleeful regret that we had to head to work again with no sleep, that the words came. We were drunk, as usual, as it had become my habit to buy a bottle of Maker's Mark for every one of our dates. Bianca was on top of me, kissing me, we were both sweaty as we had already been making love for a long time. She sat up. "Last night I had a vision, and we're going to have a baby," she said. "I dreamed that we had a baby together. We were on a road trip through the country and had stopped by the highway to walk down to the ocean. I was splashing in the water with the baby and looking back at you while you were by the car. For some reason, my friends were there too, with you, near the car. But I knew it was real. I knew it was really our baby," she said.

I knew this was just a dream. We had only been dating for a few months, and I felt so unsure of our connection the whole time. I felt like she had to be lying about something, it all seemed too good to be true. There was something about us that made the part of my brain responsible for deciding whether something was true, go off and say, "No, this isn't real." But I wanted it to be true. I wanted to think we could stay together and build a family. I had lost so many lovers, so many friends, so many possible children, so many children that I had thought I was going to have, children I had planned how to care for, children I had envisioned, children I named and dreamed of and loved before they existed, that I wanted what she was saying to be true. I ignored the part of my brain that had noticed the logical failure of the reality before me and said, "I believe you, babe. Thank you so much for telling me. That is such a beautiful vision."

She bent over me and went back to kissing me. We fucked for a long time after that. I brought her to pure bliss a few times, every time loving the fluid response from her body matching currents of neurochemicals in my brain. She couldn't bring me to that place, though, perhaps that part of my brain that I tried to ignore now wouldn't let me fully access my body and emotions after separating from it. We held each other one last time that night, but it was too late, the intensity had been too great, the interactions of chemical bonds tumbled in my brain, building to a reaction point that couldn't be stopped. As I held her, I felt her slip away. First the touch of my skin on hers and the feeling that my mind couldn't process, of our atoms touching, which they never should have. Then, the rhythm of her sleeping breath, so calm, stopped, and I was alone in bed again.

I listened to the mournful beat of an electronic song with haunting female vocals filling the darkness, the profound grief in her voice made more painful by digital filtering. As I slipped into another quantum universe, it didn't even produce an audio glitch, not a beat was lost. The transition was smooth, but I could still find differences in this new reality. I looked at the details on the print above my bed, recognizing the changes, and tears began to stream down my face. I started to move through the series of feelings that would come, sadness, denial, anger at her loss. I didn't want to accept that she was gone. I was again face to face with the truth that I couldn't get too close to anyone, or I would lose them.

Weeks later, I laid on my red couch, looking out my window at the wintery beauty of the trees, like systems of veins, the wondrous forms of evolution, and I thought of the last time I had been close to having children. Ana and I had been together for two years, and talked about having kids so many times. I had a clear vision of our daughter. It all ended so suddenly, so abruptly, like the quiet breaking of a bone.

We met at a queer performance night in Montreal. It was a long trip to travel there but I was so excited to be performing. I was in elaborate makeup with too much dark eye shadow, performing a movement piece with painful themes about my history of childhood abuse. The poem I wrote for the piece played above the melancholic, dramatic strings of an Ólafur Arnalds composition. The violin came in powerful pulses followed by sweeping arcs of agony. My movement looked strained, following rigid lines, on relevé, never quite centered. As the poem moved from painful memories to present healing, the music faded into another Arnalds song, atmospheric, with long wind sounds, fog above the ocean, punctuated by a patiently reverberating tone like an electronic bell. My strained movement became a standing pose, bent, arms flowing in waves.

After the performances, the audience chairs were removed, and the DJ played joyously danceable tunes. The kind of old hip-hop songs that you just can't resist moving to. I was still wearing my stage makeup and had thrown on a tiny nude-colored tube dress and heels. I had just gotten a drink at the bar when Ana looked at me from where she was dancing and gestured for me to join her.

I was so surprised. Ana and I had been introduced earlier by Sylvia, the dear friend who had invited me to be part of the show. As Sylvia told me of Ana's amazing activist work, I was starstruck by her femme beauty and power. I was sure she wouldn't give me the time of day.

As we danced closely, I complimented Ana's gorgeous tight, purple dress with a ribbon lacing up the back.

"Would you like to undo those ribbons," she asked, looking up at me with a flirty half smile. We went back to her apartment as snow fell. I couldn't believe I was walking through the snow in such a tiny dress and a leather jacket—all I had brought with me. I didn't have a jacket warm enough for this cold city. I was totally unprepared, in so many ways. She fed me homemade soup and informed me that she wasn't going to have sex with me. That wouldn't happen until our third date, two days later—a mistake as I always get so attached so quickly.

I was afraid she would disappear in the blink of an eye. But she didn't. We stayed together, and a few months in, we started having arguments. One day we were walking home, arguing, when she stopped.

She said, "I've just never dated anyone with a body like yours. I think it's triggering to me."

Her words wounded me. That would've been a good time for me to let things end naturally, instead of the unnatural quantum implosion my neurochemistry creates that usually tears me away from my partners. I still don't understand what happens, but I know it's anything but natural. One day I will figure it out somehow. I have to. I can't keep going in this way, losing everyone I love.

No, instead of letting things end there, I dug in deeper. I don't know why I react this way. I've lost so many people that you might think a smart survival response would be to keep my distance, cut off anyone who comes close. No. My heart and my hormones do the opposite. When things are new, I want to see everything as beautiful instead of surveying their reality. When problems arise, instead of letting them create distance, I pull closer, grasp tighter, work harder. I think, "If I can just figure this out, do the right thing, she'll stay, and I won't lose another person."

One night we were arguing over video chat, pixelated glitchy anger. It was about six months into us dating, and I wanted to call what we had a relationship. She wasn't ready. She wanted us to be dating, courting, doing cute, flirty things for each other. I was asking for a commitment, even though I was thousands of miles away, traveling to do another performance.

My insecurity won out. Or her desire to be loved won out. Or maybe her desire to feel loved, and my desire to create huge romantic gestures. She came to where I was. It seemed that we would have the romantic trip I hoped for: a weekend in Madrid thanks to cheap plane tickets and an apartment rental site. We agreed that we were in a relationship. But still, we fought bitterly through that whole trip.

We made up and made plans. I moved to her city. We went to family planning classes. We were never going to just accidentally have a child, we had to make it happen. Over brunches with some of our dearest friends, we discussed our hopes of having children and our fears. We talked about where to get sperm and whose sperm we were willing to use, and about the finances and details of how to raise children with our queer ideals. We didn't have a name for our daughter, but we did have a location for our wedding, and I could see our daughter in my mind, as clear as the morning light on that beautiful island where we were planning to be wed.

I think it was only days after the anniversary of our first date. I would like to say it was my fault and not the fault of the bizarre loophole of quantum physics that is my existence, but I don't know if that's true. In a relationship between two people, there are so many choices, so many moments where reality can split off in one direction or another, or off into both directions, in separate universes. Sometimes you can't point to a single person's decision and determine that it was their fault.

In our case, there was so much joy and so much hope, but also there was so much unhappiness. I had no idea how our lives were going to turn out. I absolutely believed that we were going to get married and have a beautiful daughter with skin the color of coffee with cream and the most gorgeous bouncy curls, spirals like the trail of an electron. I was still unsatisfied with the way we would argue so regularly. How can I analyze the trajectories of all those atoms to understand which one went the wrong direction, or if it *was* the wrong direction? It was hard to admit on a conscious, rational level that I was unhappy. I had fooled myself into believing that the problem was sex, instead of admitting that the problems were deep and myriad, that we were incompatible in so many ways.

When we first got together, I wanted everything to be beautiful, so I didn't have to withstand the pain of letting go. I let the incompatibilities pile up. I ignored them, rationalized them. Each new incompatibility I understood as a challenge that, if I was smart enough, I could defeat. I could change myself, my wants, and my needs enough to make this work because somehow leaving was wrong, staying and making it work was the only right thing to do. Of course, I was just doing what I had learned watching my mother. That no matter how drunk my father got, or what drugs he did, or even when he started selling them, she would stay, rationalize, pray things would get better. Until he left. I always understood him as the villain in that story for leaving, because he was a man and he had hurt her so badly that she completely lost touch with reality and descended into mental illness. I learned early on that to stay was noble, no matter how much it hurt, even if that hurt destroyed you. Leaving was the truly evil thing that men did, men who cheat, who leave with their mistress. I would never be like that.

So, I stayed too long. I couldn't fathom ending things. I just kept building up the fantasy of our wedding and our beautiful child. When I finally said that we should discuss our problems before the wedding, she said that I just wanted out. And she was right, even though I couldn't admit it. Or maybe she wasn't right, but the probability distribution ended up with us fighting viciously after I brought it up. Both of us crying streams of tears, she looked at me and softened.

She said, "Rea, please don't go."

Somehow this vulnerable gesture on her part helped me move out of anger and defensiveness and into openness. Still, I felt suspicious. I didn't know how we could go so quickly from fighting to touching. I always hate the scenes in movies when people argue their way into a kiss—this wasn't that scene. But it was a moment of lesbian processing slowly moving into hand holding, then into tenderness, and, soon enough, into sex. Some part of me knew that was the end, the end of our entire story, of all the friendships I had made in that story, even of my living in her snowy city. In the last few moments of our bodies touching, the last few moments of our time together, I rolled over onto my back, and everything slipped, like a glitch in a digital video but instead the whole world glitched. I was back in Los Angeles, in the guest bedroom of my best friend, Ricardo, and his partner. The warm night held the sound of insects outside the open window. The grief hit so hard; no astronomical instruments would be able to measure its force. I knew that everything that had happened now only existed in the folds of my memory.

CHAPTER 3.

Cora ran through the decisions she made that led her to this airport, to do this hack, as the boarding announcement for her flight flashed in her view. Each of those decisions was a point of divergence that could create a different universe. She turned away from the mirror. She had formulated the plan two weeks ago. She had been so triggered by the election of such a vile, racist, misogynist that she was dissociating, going through her days in a haze, mechanically doing the tasks required for survival, like eating and showering. Finally, the last thread supporting her sense that participation in a life accepted as normal—one with a day job, a salary and credit cards—could lead to safety broke.

She had been eating pad thai in a restaurant she liked, still too despondent about the election to cook for herself, while watching the news. Images of the rapist-elect waving, smiling, and speaking in front of Congress played on the flat-screen television on the wall. He declared, again, that immigrants are criminals, drug dealers, and rapists. Text scrolled below his horrific face: "Final sexual assault victim settles out of court, President-elect pays undisclosed sum."

In that moment, she decided that she could not be a part of a society that accepted this president's lies as facts. Eighteen women had publicly declared that this man had sexually assaulted them, and their truths had been flatly denied. She had held out some hope that the multiple reports might come to something, might cause him to be charged with a crime, and might prevent him from taking office. Yet as these cases faded into the background, the truth that he was taking power over the country became undeniable. She felt profound rage, terror, and grief all at once that made her face feel hot. That's when she made her decision.

She walked away from Omelas—as Le Guin would say—away from her life of normalcy and back to the life of a hacker. She opened two virtual windows in her aug overlaying the scene of the Thai restaurant and began to set up the hack. Looking to the left of the augmented reality interface, she proceeded to book a plane ticket, then looking slightly to the right of that window, she fired up her Internet Relay Chat (IRC) client in a terminal and sent a message out from her handle, diosa_andriode.

#TbitchIRC: 1143:: @diosa_andriode: Need accounts. Have cc's to trade.

#TbitchIRC: :: @nepantla: msg me.

Cora had been a hacker long enough to know what they want, credit card numbers to use online. With the advent of bitcoin and darknets, they can order literally anything they could want, whether legal or not, drugs, ghost guns—anything. She also remembered some of her old favorite spots to meet other black hats and exchange card login and password combinations: a fairly obscure, text-based chat system, where users can create private servers and private channels with just a few keystrokes. Well, it might not be as obscure anymore, after a famous, heroic trans woman shared US military secrets and endured a trial that included IRC transcripts. But the platform was certainly still hard enough to use that it had not gained in popularity—why would anyone not in search of anonymity want to use a text-based chat client when they have voice messaging instead?

Within twenty minutes of her chat with nepantla, as she was finishing her duck curry, she had obtained a few logins for shell accounts on servers in various parts of the world. She was willing to hand over her own credit card numbers to a random hacker to get accounts she could use to hack the criminal records system. These were credit cards that she had opened over the last few years working as a software engineer, which meant taking a big step away from her current professional life in this moment. After discussing the details of her credit limits and lying about the origin of the cards, she reached for her purse to give nepantla the actual numbers. Leaning over, she felt it again, like the world slowly, slightly tilted forward too far. Or it was she who continued tilting forward and the world stood still. Either way, there was that slight feeling again, a slow spinning. The fear of realizing it was happening dropping out of her stomach, and then the flicker and reset of her vision, like she had lost just a small millisecond of time.

Fuck. Is it my auglenses? Or is it my inner ear, like the doctor said? Is it going to get worse? thought Cora.

She'd turned back to her keyboard, pulled her wallet out of her bag, and resumed her plan. She double checked the other aug window with a turn of her head to the left, to make sure her plane ticket booking had gone through, and it had.

Cora came out of that memory into the tense reality of the airport bathroom. Leaving the bathroom, Cora took her backpack and rolling carry on and headed toward the gate. She began to feel fear weighing on her chest. She knew that going back to Bogotá, Colombia, would involve extra security screenings, but that was where she wanted to end up if she was going to have to go underground. Also, she knew that a long flight across that many latitude lines would require the plane's Wi-Fi connection to change satellites multiple times, making her even less trackable. She wasn't fully aware of it, but her breathing was becoming shallower. All the muscles in her chest and upper back were tightening and her gait shifted, too, her steps becoming just slightly smaller than usual as she walked up to the TSA checkpoint at the entry to gate C39 for the flight to Bogotá.

She always held fear in her chest and in her lower torso, in her lower abs, glutes, and adductors, the places where she had been harmed the most. Years of therapy had helped her know this, had started to release those muscles. But in times like these, her amygdala flooded her body with cortisol and norepinephrine, a response that started with childhood trauma and were ingrained later through sexual assault.

"Bags through the scanner. Take off all metal items. Place your items in a bin," said the female Transportation Security Agency agent. She was a Korean woman, probably in her late twenties. She gave instructions to Cora with a lack of enthusiasm that spoke of her own disdain for the job she was doing or maybe just the boredom of the monotonous repetition. Cora couldn't muster anger at her; she knew that jobs were scarce, and people of color are often made to do the work of structural racism through economic coercion. You have to make a living, even if it means carrying out the physical labor of injustice in a country that just upvoted Islamophobia, xenophobia, and racism in the form of a president who'd announced he planned to do all he could to keep Muslim, Latinx, and Haitian immigrants from entering the country. Cora took off her coat, put her bag containing her laptop on the belt, and glanced at the white male TSA agent sitting next to the scanner poring over its readings that only he could see in his auglenses. He was dutiful, attentive, like he believed in what he was doing.

"Laptop" was just a euphemism, an outdated word still used for a technology that did not sit on your lap. Cora's "laptop" was just a battery, a small flash storage device with a 250-petabyte capacity, sensor package, and transmitter package in the size and shape of a tube of lipstick. It needed to rest somewhere near your lap to be able to measure the movement of your fingers for the aug keyboard, a virtual keyboard that you only see in your auglenses. The laptop was capable of connecting to cellular networks, Wi-Fi, Bluetooth, and NFC, which was how the auglenses interfaced to her laptop. As she watched her bags make their way down the belt, she felt fear, but she was prepared for this moment, prepared for the checkpoint, so the feeling didn't progress to terror. She knew the difference well, the gradations of fear and terror, living life as a trans woman of color and a survivor.

While the multiscanners were standard across airports, she knew that at this gate, going to Colombia, the agents were focused on looking for drugs. That wasn't what worried her; she didn't have drugs on her, only malicious code. She watched her bag slide into the multiscanner.

The multiscanner was the product of a profitable collaboration between law enforcement and information technology companies. It was capable of X-raying bags that passed through and conducted digital X-rays, or DX-rays, that read the information on any devices stored inside. The TSA had mandated that laptops taken aboard airplanes had to be compliant with the NFC wireless DX-ray standard that facilitated quick analysis of the data they contained. In recent years, these industries had found a way to profit off of looking like they were trying to stop the passage of digital contraband; they claimed to have the capacity to identify munitions-grade encryption, illegal forms of pornography, and pirated copies of copyrighted media.

Cora had researched this multiscanner and knew it well. She knew that no algorithm could comb through all of 250 petabytes in just a few seconds. Instead, the DX-ray took a random sampling of sectors from the flash drive and analyzed its contents by comparing them against known data formats. With that knowledge, she had written a program to smuggle the malicious software tools she needed onto the plane.

A few days before coming to the airport, she had prepared by downloading the latest VR experience of underwater diving in cenotes in Tulum, Mexico. She took only a few minutes to watch and enjoy the feeling of swimming through a cavern so large a blue whale could swim in it, her flashlight creating a clear beam through the water whose shades of zaffer, midnight, and indigo indicated layers of pressure and depth awaiting her. Great—the file was good, terabytes of data downloaded properly in just a few minutes.

Many VR experiences are basically video, actually a series of videos, that shows the same segment of time from multiple angles, allowing you to feel immersed in a wholly different scene, seeing other perspectives through your auglenses as you turn your head. The way video data compression works is by having a standard for the data that defines the header and the frames of video, as well as instructions for each frame and instructions that carry across frames. Her program used this format to hide her software by embedding it in two ways into the VR file to make sure the TSA's algorithms couldn't find her Wi-Fi cracking software.

Software can be looked at as text. Imagine that a single program, like a word processor or music player, contains about as much text as a 300-page book. Usually, it exists as binary code in a file that gets executed by the processor of your computer. If you open that file in a text editor, you see lines and lines of junk characters as the text editor tries to convert this linear data into character sets readable by humans. Cora's program started by cutting the software into small pieces, like pages of a book. Each page was then stuffed into a single frame of the VR video. The format for encoding these videos, in this case as mp5, has a few bytes defined in the header of each frame to allow for a comment, which is often used to include things like decoding instructions or watermarks. Cora exploited this comment area to hide small parts of the tools she needed in each frame of the cave-diving video, thus making her code virtually invisible to algorithmic data scanners like the DX-ray.

But to be more thorough, she took some of the remaining data that made up her software program and concealed it even further. She used the instructions that cross frames—instructions like, "Keep this background pixel at gray shade #221711 for the next twenty frames"—to hide both the rest of her program's data and an encryption key. In this way she could store all of the code in each frame of the video, encrypted, along with the decryption code, just to confuse simple analyses. The result was that playing the mp5 file, would plunge you into a VR experience of underwater cave diving in Tulum Cenotes, with only the slightest glitch every few minutes where a part of the video stayed in place for perhaps a millisecond too long. This meant that, for the most part, her data was hidden from both computer forensic techniques and the human eye.

She stepped through the millimeter wave radiation scanner. The female agent said, "Go ahead." The body scan was the easy part, now, post-op. Cora then walked up and stood next to the multiscanner, waiting for her bag to come out. Far off at the edge of her awareness, she felt the tightness in her chest and abs. She knew that if they found something they were suspicious of, they would pull her bag off the belt instead of sending it through.

Her eyes rested on the white male agent. He was in his early forties, it seemed. His dry hair, a vague shade of brownish yellow, brushed to the side, his brown eyes fixed on the image from the multiscanner appearing in his auglenses. Surely his auglenses had particular enhancements that allowed him to see the multiple spectrums beyond color that the multiscanner relied on to convey the calculations it made about the contents of the bag and devices, including their chemical compositions, temperatures, amount of atomic movement, and the machine's estimations of the accuracy of its findings. Cora waited, as the agent used his hand to zoom in on part of the image. She noticed how he moved his neck as if to draw closer to the image though this wasn't needed with auglenses; it was a residual habit from his early years of screen usage.

The time flashed again in her auglenses, seeming to float in the air next to the head of the TSA agent on whom her attention was so fixed.

1:00, final boarding for Flight 305 to Bogotá

00:59, final boarding for Flight 305 to Bogotá

00:58, final boarding for Flight 305 to Bogotá

With the slightest tilt of his head for Cora to go through, the moment ended. The belt moved along with a hum and Cora's backpack, with its familiar red and black ballistic nylon, and her purple rolling carry on came out of the scanner. She picked them up, strode toward the gate and felt some of her muscles relax slightly. She took a deep breath and sighed hard; her body noticed the lack of oxygen from her shallow breathing even if she hadn't.

The gate agent was scanning in the last two passengers ahead of Cora. One by one they stepped into place and stood still in front of the agent in her navy-blue uniform with crimson accents on the lapel, who evaluated each passenger with her auglens. In her vision, she saw the display of the passenger's name, gender, seat number, class, and security threat level, which in most cases was simply a line of green text below the passenger's information saying, "Welcome." Only a few times since training had that line changed to the red "Please step aside," and she had not noticed that most often those passengers were Muslim women in headscarves. Cora stood in line behind the two passengers, an older couple chattering with joy about going home to Colombia. Both had gray hair. They walked through the door to the jet bridge with difficulty, the woman holding onto the man's arm for balance.

Cora stepped into place. The agent had only to look at her to scan her for boarding. As the agent's eyes rested on Cora, she looked at the agent and tried to smile. Her mind quickly traveled over the subtle modifications to her body that were the results of her gender confirmation surgery. In addition to the more traditional changes to the body to match one's desired gender characteristics, doctors had developed a way to allow trans people to register digitally as their chosen gender, given the ubiquity of gender detection algorithms. Medical researchers worked with computer science researchers to understand the algorithms that calculated gender in auglenses, on social media, and in surveillance systems. These gender-analysis algorithms relied on a series of checks that set flags, variables used to count the number of characteristics that matched coded gender standards.

A few tiny imperfections could be added to the skin that were invisible to the naked eye, but were visible to charged coupled devices (CCDs)—the retinas of digital cameras. Using a fine laser, the surgeon introduced tiny incisions that, when healed, became indentations that introduced the slightest amount of shadow. These new minuscule shadows were placed in important locations for the algorithmic analysis of gender: on the border zones between major bodily features, such as between shoulder and collarbone. If enough ambiguity or error was introduced into the evaluation of the first flag, such as jaw shape, then that error was incorporated as a heuristic into the evaluation of the next flag. The error carried through and accumulated. As the algorithm moved on to evaluate the shape of a person's shoulders as male or female, if the previous calculation of jaw shape had enough ambiguity, then the shoulder calculation could be affected. Through this cascade of errors introduced at certain points in the algorithm, the resulting gender outcome could be modified. By doing so, trans people could be assured that not only did their physical anatomy match their felt sense of gender, but the scanners they passed through on a daily basis to validate their identity for security cameras, legal identification, and even when paying for their groceries at the store, would register their gender in congruence with their legal documents and allow them to continue daily life unimpeded.

The algorithms inside the gate agent's auglens analyzed Cora, her shape, her color, her degree of movement, her pulse as perceptible by its movement under the skin on her neck, and the tightness of her chest and torso, as her body swayed ever so slightly, the closest to stillness she could get. A subroutine for checking stress detected Cora's heart rate as far above the normal range. The subroutine determined that she had either ran at her maximum capacity to the gate, or she was lying. As a result, the gate agent said, "Just a moment, ma'am," as her laptop's wireless connection quickly fired out a request for and received Cora's medical information. The stress subroutine evaluated Cora's answers about her medical history that she had willingly supplied to TSA in order to register for Transparent Traveler and make her business travel as a software engineer less difficult.

In that moment, Cora looked past the gate agent to the jetway, and at the bright, electric pink sunset blooming above the movement of the tails of passenger jets. She thought of how it reminded her of sunrise in bed with Juana. Of all the good things in her life, cuddling with Juana, just being two people cozy under the sheets together on a cold morning, waking up to the joy of feeling the soft warmth of another's skin on yours, seemed like something worth fighting for and something that still might be possible in this world, if she could get through this last checkpoint.

The subroutine compared her medical history against a list of possible reasons for an elevated heart rate, such as high cholesterol, heart disease, hypertension. Finding that she had reported a diagnosis of Complex Post-Traumatic Stress Disorder, the subroutine was satisfied. The subroutine determined that Cora's elevated heart rate was justified by her C-PTSD diagnosis and returned that information to the main program that had called on it to evaluate whether Cora should be let on the plane. "Welcome," said the agent with a smile, "We hope you enjoy your flight on Pacifica Airlines." Cora stepped onto the jet bridge, about to pull off a hack that would change history, and she didn't even notice her upper back and her stomach muscles relax, ever so slightly.

CHAPTER 4.

I found myself back in Los Angeles after losing another love. I lost so many people that I began trying to study why and how reality could change in front of my eyes. I learned about quantum physics but not enough to know what was going on with me. I read books by Neil deGrasse Tyson, Stephen Hawking, Richard Feynman, Carlo Rovelli, and Chanda Prescod-Weinstein. I understood some of the principles, but not enough of the chemistry. More importantly, I needed a hacker.

For months, I had been working on a mathematical model of what I thought was going on with me, but I needed someone who could help me code a simulation of it. I could write a good poem or create a dance performance, but my algorithm looked more like a recipe with symbols for differential equations and formulas for derivatives scribbled down the sides. To really get at what was going on, I would need a coder who could help me visualize the complexity of unfolding universes and how my oxytocin production could possibly be tied to my own causal timeline.

These thoughts came to me as I lay on my couch, watching sideways images of the terrifying reality of fascism expanding across the US. I rarely watched television, mostly preferring shows on video streaming services where I could find lesbian-centered stories that I could actually relate to. After living in my friend's guest room for a few months while I recovered from depression, I had finally found a job at a local community college teaching introductory composition classes to frosh. It allowed me a lot of room to teach what I wanted, so I often had my students doing movement performances with text, which they felt shy about, but I found an important way to think through my own creative work. Above all, the job allowed me to save enough money to move into my own apartment. Fortunately, the shift to this new reality maintained some of my timeline intact, my friendship with Ricardo, my knowledge of poetry and dance.

Ricardo and his partner were as surprised as I was that I had shown up at their house, but when he saw my tears, he knew it was heartbreak that had brought me. He just didn't know about the wormhole that my heartbreak had created, so I left out a lot of the details of where I had been living and who with when I shared the story. Ricardo looked at me with the usual warm, compassionate, patient eyes with which he always met my sadness. Over the years, I had come to appreciate his capacity for listening and his gentleness so profoundly, as he had held space for me in more than one of these moments of grief so intense that it tears the bonds of my molecules.

In my new apartment, by myself, I missed Ricardo. My couch was not very comfortable, but I was happy to have a couch that was my own. My apartment had a small view of the ocean, so I put the couch next to the window where I could sit and see it. That night, I lay on the couch with tears streaming from my eyes, watching a fascist be elected president of the United States. I did not expect this. I had followed the news, all eighteen of the reports from women insisting that he had assaulted them. I had read the details of their accounts, even the woman who said she was only a child when he'd assaulted her. There was no way he could be elected, I thought. I was so triggered by even the thought that a rapist was still a candidate for the presidency that I spent the weeks leading up to the election in a haze of fear and mild panic. Now, that panic was morphing into an outpouring of tears down my face. I stayed up late watching the expressions of shock, disbelief, and sadness on the news reporters' faces echoing my own. No one could believe that this violent, terrible autocrat was being elected, but he was. After 1:15 a.m., he walked onto the stage to announce that he had defeated his female opponent in the election, a victory for racists everywhere.

The next day, I was devastated. After so many months of healing from intense loss, after trying so hard to regain my sense of self, why had I slipped into this horrific dystopian timeline? It felt profoundly unfair. I did not believe in any god, but I did believe that for all the effort put into quantum physics, cosmology, and theoretical physics, these explanations still could not account for most of the workings of the miracles that are our universes. But that day, I was even furious at the universe. How could this unprecedented surge of hate be the unfolding spirit of the universe?

Nothing made sense. My hope at finding any answers about myself was lost in the sudden incomprehensibility of the people around me, half of whom had voted for this violent, misogynist buffoon. I received a text from my dear friend Xandra: "Hey Rea, come join me downtown at the protest. We're at Figueroa and Pico!" I canceled my classes and drove to meet her. I couldn't be alone, crying on my couch; I had to be with people. I was grateful to be in a city with so many other Latinx people. It was a city where the election of this man who had associated our people with rapists, when he himself was one, was met with massive outrage. People were flooding the streets en masse, waving Mexican flags, covering their faces with bandannas, driving lowriders alongside the march.

We marched for hours, keeping our chants simple for all the people who were there marching for the first time and didn't know the more fun but more elaborate beats of chants from other movements. When Xandra had to leave, I stayed with the march. We marched up and down hills, the march leaders routing around the police whenever they tried to stop our march at an intersection. At one point, deep in downtown, on Flower and Eleventh, we could see the lights of police cars coming from far away, slowly, as we realized another march with hundreds of people in it was marching toward our contingent to join us! Our march was already around a thousand people strong before even stopping to allow them to come down Eleventh and merge with ours.

My voice was hoarse from chanting. The march had been so impulsive that no one had even brought a bullhorn. These were not experienced organizers so much as they were people who had thought that activism was hopeless until now. Maybe they still thought it was hopeless, but there seemed to be a collective need to scream and cry, in public, together.

That's when I noticed her also standing just outside the crowd. A Latina woman whose muscular, tattoo-covered arms were revealed by her Black Lives Matter t-shirt, the sleeves of which she had stylishly cut off herself. Flowers trailed down her gorgeous brown arms, connected by curves resembling the traces of particles like pions, the result of high-speed collisions produced in accelerators and supernovas, which exist only briefly when a high energy proton collides with another particle. I felt myself still in that moment as I looked at her. Her eyes locked on the police; she was wearing ear buds. Her eyes were glassy like she was looking at something I couldn't see, and her fingers were twitching busily. It looked like she was using an invisible keyboard—surely, she had auglenses and was recording this entire scene. The rays of light and shadow scanning across her body alternated from red to blue and white, creating a cacophony of angles that she seemed unmoved by. Her beauty was unfolding in my consciousness as I noticed how close she was standing to the police, even as they were violently pushing people back with their electric bicycles. She was close enough to see their badge numbers—or at least those whose badge numbers were not covered with black tape, as most were that night.

The chanting, the sirens, and the helicopter all faded away as she held a stillness that mirrored my own. In the many worlds interpretation of quantum mechanics, many of the impossibilities that quantum mechanics presents, such as action at a distance and the uncertainty of particle locations, are solved by the idea that in any quantum experiment with multiple possible outcomes, all outcomes exist in different universes. Quantum entanglement is the phenomenon of two particles that can be separated across vast distances and yet the quantum states of one particle still correlate to changes in the other. Einstein referred to this as spooky action at a distance.

Almost any event can be a quantum experiment, such as a flickering lightbulb as evidence that even light exists in packets or quanta. Still, moments like this one have always felt to me like experiments of particular relevance. How can we ever know all the possible outcomes and variables that contributed to the meeting of two people? What quantum effects happen in the moment when the police car's red light flashes off her body and sends that image to my brain, resulting in this powerful attraction? What patterns of shape, like the movement of her hair, reach the neural networks in my hippocampus, interact with my memory, and create this feeling of warmth down my body? How does the context of this political moment, and her act of resistance within it, register in that pattern recognition and interact with all the work I've done on myself to heal and build healthy relationship patterns in such a way that I decide to walk toward her?

When the moment of police violence subsides back into the baseline tension of a police line standing at the ready, holding their e-bikes as weapons waiting to be used again, I said to her over the din of the protest, "Hey, thanks, for documenting."

She looked at me, surprised, and gave me a slight, nervous smile, "Yeah, it's important! These fuckers might go off at any moment!"

"Yeah . . . Ahh, can we be buddies? My friend had to go home, and I don't know anyone else at this protest. Also, it looks like you could use someone to watch your back if you're going to keep recording them."

"Ah, yeah, cool. Thanks!"

"Me llamo Realidad—I'm Realidad. You can call me Rea."

"I'm Cora. ¡Mucho gusto!" she replied.

When the feeder march arrived and joined our group, everyone erupted into cheers, our cries bouncing off the LA skyscrapers, up past the police helicopter, and toward the night sky. The march continued, and Cora and I stayed together.

"You seem like you know what you're doing," I said to Cora.

"Yeah, I've been out here with Black Lives Matter so many times this year. I'm tired. I'm just so fucking tired."

"I hear you. I haven't had the energy to come out and protest much because the news has been so depressing," I said. "I really admire that people have been out here day after day. And now things are even worse."

"It was a devastating year. Every time I open my Metatext app, it seems like another Black person or another trans sister has been murdered. I can't keep doing it. I've been staying off social media lately. Even before this nightmare election, more trans women had been murdered this year than ever before," she said and looked at me to gauge my response. I looked her in the eyes, knowing that grief so well, trying to communicate that to her.

"I know," was all I could get out as I shook my head, wrinkled my brow, and almost started to cry but held it in to continue marching. "I've been spending all my time journaling, talking to friends, learning to take care of myself. It's been all I could do to survive," I said. She looked me back in the eyes, echoing the feeling that pain had taken her to her limit, too.

We marched for over an hour, snaking through downtown, until we arrived at the tracks of the Metro Rail, where the march stopped. The crowd split once people realized that this was a turning point. Most stepped away from the tracks—a train was approaching with its headlights on. Still, a group of at least fifty of us stayed on the tracks. The police lined up at a distance. I saw Cora pause and look away, as if she was listening in to something in her earbud. She rushed toward a Black trans woman wearing a kaffiyeh and a backpack over to our right, touched her shoulder, and said, "The riot cops and paddy wagon are on their way. They were staging just a few blocks up."

As the Metro train drew closer and slowed to a crawl, the police announced over their loudspeaker, "THIS IS AN UNLAWFUL ASSEMBLY. ANYONE WHO DOES NOT DISPERSE IMMEDIATELY WILL BE SUBJECT TO ARREST. I REPEAT: THIS IS AN UNLAWFUL ASSEMBLY. ANYONE WHO DOES NOT DISPERSE IMME-DIATELY WILL BE SUBJECT TO ARREST."

The woman who Cora had spoken to and a few other organizers who had made speeches earlier at the rally looked around at all of us and started yelling, "SIT DOWN! SIT DOWN!" gesturing with their hands for us to do so. My heart was pounding. I took out my phone and began recording video as the police line moved closer to us. The sound of the heli-copter got louder as it circled right above us. I looked at Cora. She looked determined and aware, but I could still see the fear there. She must have known as well as I did what would happen to girls like us in jail. I imagined she also felt the daily threat of violence, wondering if she would come back home each night as she left her home each morning, and I felt deeply protective of her. I moved closer, crouching like she was, not sitting, ready to move if necessary.

The train slowed to a stop with a loud screeching sound. We were interrupting business as usual. How many more Metro trains around the city were also now stopped because of this one? The organizers knew that Metro Rail was a point of infrastructure that could be targeted in order to disrupt traffic across many intersections around Los Angeles, not just this one. The police knew it too and was why they were slapping their billy clubs against their palms, raising their cans of pepper spray at us. Time seemed to slow, as I looked nervously from Cora to the police to the organizers, seeing who would move first. The stopped train was blaring its horn at us.

After what felt like hours but was surely only a few minutes, the riot police arrived and poured out of their vans, tens of them, carrying rubber bullet rifles in the ready position, rifle butts against their shoulders, their plastic face shields down making them look more menacing. They filled the space between the line of street cops and the group of protesters sitting on the Metro tracks. Behind us the larger crowd from the march chanted, "WHOSE STREETS? OUR STREETS!" alternating with, "NO COPS! NO KKK! NO FASCIST USA!"

The police started another announcement, so piercingly loud it must have been announced through their long-range acoustic device (LRAD), their sound weapon, and not from a police car loudspeaker. "THIS IS YOUR FINAL WAR—"

The organizers, now in a small huddle, burst upright and began walking quickly away from the cops, shouting, "GO! LET'S GO! COME ON!" I finally breathed and grabbed Cora's arm.

"Come on!" I said. She looked at me with surprise but responded by pulling closer to me as we walked at a fast pace away from the tracks, the cops, and their guns. The march leaders had made a tactical decision to continue snaking through downtown, continuing the disruption of traffic for hours, rather than concede this single point of congestion and have to deal with a lot of arrests and injuries. And they didn't want to allow the cops the satisfaction of finishing their sentence, preferring to interrupt their futile announcement. The time for that kind of escalation would come, but it wasn't tonight.

Afterward, Cora and I sat in a Oaxacan restaurant near her apartment on Venice Boulevard. The ceiling was covered in the curved garlands of paper flags intricately cut into grids, skulls, skeletons, and flowers, in the brightest teals, pinks, and reds, with some cut from foil for even more sparkle. The fat horn notes and rapidly tumbling accordion sounds of Norteño music unfolded in the background. I ate my favorite mole negro con pollo, a specialty Oaxaqueño, and sipped on my horchata. Cora sat sideways, her back to the wall and feet up on the seat of the booth we were in.

She hummed loudly, "MMMMM . . . chile relleno!" Oaxacan cheese is famously creamy, and the stuffed chiles were a rich delight after so much marching. She was even indulging in a Mexican hot chocolate to go with it, a complex flavor of cinnamon and cacao, to celebrate surviving the night.

"So, how did you know that the riot cops were on their way?" I asked.

"Well . . . " Cora stalled and smiled slyly, shifting her eyes to the side.

"I mean, of course we all knew that the riot cops would be there any minute, but you knew more than that. It really helped us hold the space longer," I said.

"I've done comms for protests in the past and for direct actions. When I was eight years old, my dad was put in prison on charges of selling cocaine that he said he was framed for.

I always knew the police were the enemy, even before I had prison abolitionist or anti-colonial politics. It's not difficult to get police scanners, but they're clunky, heavy radios. What's better is to pick up on an mp3 stream of a police scanner signal. You can find them online for most large cities easily enough. Sometimes even news websites post links to them. I just pulled it up on my phone and brought my wireless earbuds with me. On top of the audio signal, there's a separate channel for digital data that the cops also use for dispatching. I can see all of that in my auglenses."

"You have auglenses?" I asked.

"Yeah, I'm a coder and 3D designer, so I kind of have to have them for work. At the protest, I could see the red and orange heat signatures and the heartrates of each officer, so I could estimate who might shoot first. My auglenses are even high enough resolution to record the serial numbers on all of their weapons, too. And with the data channel paralleling the radio dispatch, I could see who was talking at any moment, while my heads-up display showed me a purple map overlay of all other police cars in the area, and their velocities, by their GPS locations. It's still pretty disorienting, as I just got these augs, so I can't keep them turned on all the time. I wish I could show you what I can see. It's like a dancing web of spinning lines and curved trajectories across the whole spectrum of color. But you can hear the radio channel. Here," she said, as she handed me the earbud and pulled out her phone.

I heard static, a squeal, then a female voice saying, "10 7 7 15 5 77. I copy. Do you need the return?"

"No, ma'am," replied a male voice, then said, "Can you have 1141 respond to our location? Thirty-five-year-old male with bruising."

Another voice then, "Information only 21–23. Driver on Rosecrans speeding, cutting people off."

I noticed music behind the chatter, a slow, rising electronic tone, echoing, resonating, shimmering.

"Now do you copy, 1693?"

The reverbed sound continued when the voice stopped, changing to a continuous high-pitched note then slowly resonating, stopping, and replaced with a pulsing mid-range A2 note. It lent a peaceful undertone to the scanner, turning it all into a kind of music. Then the high note again, and a male voice: "LA 95, cancel our squad request."

"Copy. Request canceled for Sepulveda," the female voice responded.

I glanced at Cora's phone on the table next to her hand. It showed an image of sunset over Los Angeles, the city viewed from far above. To the left, lines of traffic and streetlights receding into the distance, forming sharp angles. To the right, glowing orange horizon, clouds, and gray-blue fading into night. The text across the top read, *YOU ARE LISTENING TO LOS ANGELES.*

I took the earbud out of my ear and looked back at Cora, who was smiling flirtatiously, head tilted back. "Nice, huh? Some radio geek keeps that site up so you can load the scanner feed with music and just listen all night long. Do you want to come over and listen to the city with me?"

Smiling back, such a big smile I had to hold back a giggle. I wasn't expecting this, and I was flattered. "That's a very enticing offer, and I would love to, but not yet. I would like to see you again, though, very much. For a less chaotic date," I said.

CHAPTER 5.

Cora was so gorgeous, but I had a plan. I did not want to dive into the matrix of yet another fast-paced relationship that ended in crushing heartbreak. I was going to take my sweet time with Cora. Maybe if I could approach my relationships in a more grounded way and kept my feelings growing at a healthier pace, just maybe my neurochemistry wouldn't tear me out of this universe again. I hoped so, a deep longing hope. Maybe this time I would be able to stay. But the only way to test that was if I didn't get too attached immediately. So, I refused to spin off into hopes and fantasies about Cora. I needed to stay in the moment, move slowly, and avoid a chain reaction.

Cora and I agreed to go on another date a week from the night we met. Part of my plan was no kissing on the first date, and that had been hard enough to hold myself to when she'd invited me to her place at the Oaxacan restaurant. I talked to my dear friend Xandra about my plan, to try to keep myself accountable. Our idea for our second date was to go see a science fiction movie. It seemed safe enough, while still getting to be in the dark together. But I was too excited to be able to decide what to wear. I wanted to wear something hot but not too revealing, something tight in some places but loose in others that would communicate that I want to take it easy and go slow. I went with a casual black dress with small white polka dots, below the knee but with a nice low neckline. It turned out that I didn't even have to say it; Cora told me first that she wanted to date very intentionally and take her time to get to know me. I explained in glee that I wanted the same thing! After the date, I called Xandra to check in and bookend that I had held my boundaries. She was happy to hear it and proud of me.

For our third date, Cora and I went to the sculpture park by the bay, just before sunset. We strolled around the sculptures, marveling at them, critiquing them, laughing at them, alternately in awe of their beauty and bored by their banality. After that, we laid on a hill and watched the sun's blazing fusion reactions light up the bay, the sky, and the clouds with a slow, spectral dance of fiery orange and rose fading into magenta.

Cora told me that she'd had surgery about six months before we met. She was in between finishing one job and starting another, and her partner had broken up with her just a month before her surgery. The combination of paying for surgery with all its related costs, like prescriptions, lots of meals ordered out, and travel to the Bay Area city where she received her surgery, on top of having to move out of the apartment she shared with her partner, had drained all her savings. As a result, she had ended up living with her brother and his partner for months afterward.

Recovery from surgery was brutal, Cora explained. The first week she couldn't see, her eyes were still adjusting to the auglenses, and she could barely walk. For the first few days after surgery, they kept her eyes bandaged while her corneas healed. She had to accept help from the hospital staff and her friends just to move around her hospital room. Over the week, she gradually built up enough strength to walk around her floor of the hospital and could see through blurry vision. She had to stay medicated on painkillers constantly, which made her nauseous and constipated, in addition to putting her into a mental haze. After a few weeks, once she could focus her eyes again, she tried to pass the days watching streaming television but interesting movies, like David Lynch's *Dune*, were too complex for her to follow. She had to default to watching base reality shows, hours of *So You Think You Can Dance*. Cora loved dancing, boxing, cycling, running, any kind of physical activity, which eased her ADHD and released some of her anxious energy. She could do none of those things now. Turning on her auglenses was still completely disorienting—it felt like a blast of color and light directly to her retinas that hurt like an intense headache.

After a few weeks, she tried to wean herself off the pre-scribed oxycodone so that she could get her mind back. But she could only take a maximum number of Advil or Tylenol each day without damaging her liver. Her mind was too blurry to keep track of what she had taken so she kept a journal. It would take months for her to heal and adjust to her new body and her new senses. She had just gotten the body she had wished for her whole life, but she was the most depressed she had ever been. While Cora was speaking, the sun had long ago gone down.

"It's hard for me to tell you all this. Are you sure you want to hear more? It got much worse before it got better," Cora said to me with vulnerability in her eyes.

"You can share as much as you want with me. I'm so hon-ored to witness your story," I said and touched her hand. We both looked at the white moonlight on the water, billions of photons reflecting the sun, cooled by the cold surface of the moon, distilled into a dancing waveform before us.

"After months of recovery, including three months of lying down and slowly regaining the use of my eyes, I was at the lowest point I had ever been. I need to move my body to feel good. And I get a lot of self-worth from my work. Not being able to do much of anything for so long made me feel sad and worthless. It was rough."

Once she was healed enough to have sex, Cora decided to try online dating. She installed the app on her phone and connected it to her auglenses with NFC wireless communication. The old manner of swiping left or right had given way to a simple head movement to the right or left to see the next person's profile, and a nod to acknowledge that you wanted to connect with that person. Sitting on the bed in her brother's guest bedroom, gesturing no, no, no through so many profiles, and yes to a few, she received a message. It was from a cute femme in glasses and a yellow dress, all frill and ruffles. Her name, Lily, hovered over her image. She was beaming a saccharine smile.

Cora wasn't very interested in her, she told me, but the message had immediately lifted her spirits. After months of depression, she suddenly felt warm, attractive, happy. The note was short, saying that she always liked a hot femme like Cora and that she'd love to get together some time. Cora read her profile and it was intense: behind that sweet smile, Lily said she was into roleplay, which made Cora wonder if they'd be compatible, since she was not. But she thought to deal with that later if it came up. Cora messaged her, and they agreed on a cute date the next day at a gelato place near where Cora was staying.

Standing on the corner near the gelato place, among gleaming exotic cars driving through Culver City, just blocks away from the big film studios, the sun shone hot that summer day. Lily crossed the street to Cora, and they immediately laughed and hugged. Lily pulled away from the hug slowly, seeming to almost kiss Cora, and Cora felt like there was instant electricity. Actually, she had been so sad that, this contrast, this moment of light and appreciation made her serotonin flow hard. Instead of finding it strange that Lily had so few boundaries with an almost complete stranger, Cora thought it was a magical connection. Cora liked that she was clearly about the same age, in her late thirties, but with an ageless quality that reminded her of her mother. Cora wore a short mint-colored dress that day, with shoulder straps and a slight A-line. They walked into the store together and ordered gelato. They went on a few more dates and had sex.

After that, Cora didn't hear from Lily for weeks. She sent her a message through the dating app and got a reply that Lily wasn't interested in seeing her again. That was enough to send Cora even deeper into depression. She felt used and stupid. She felt like she had learned a lesson in being a woman with a vagina: that she was now desirable, but as an object. As she talked to her friends, she realized that people basically "shop for sex" through online dating apps and felt even more stupid. Her new job was still a month away from starting, but now Cora was in a deep depression. She ate huge chocolate bars and wondered why she couldn't sleep. She cried all night for weeks. Finally, she got an emergency appointment with a psychiatrist and was put on antidepressants.

She asked for medication that would be sedating in order to help her sleep and was given Remeron. She was grateful that the Remeron dulled the world and made her memory fuzzy. When Cora looked in the mirror at her expressionless face, she knew she couldn't stay on the Remeron when she started her new job, but for now, it allowed her to sleep.

By now, five months after surgery, her auglenses were healed and her retinas had adjusted to their intensity. She began to be able to use them without the excruciating pain that they had occasioned, and she could now start learning to operate them. She began with a simple calibration exercise, which her augmentation therapist told her to do every day. Turning on her auglenses by blinking in the correct pattern, which she had previously chosen, she brought up the calibration program.

Using her fingers to zoom, she set a tiny red dot at the center of her vision, as a circle and crosshairs that she was using to make the exercise simpler appeared to float between her and the wall. Cora moved her head, and the dot moved, but the crosshairs stayed still. She tried to move the dot along the crosshairs and then along the circle that encompassed it, which was a challenge. She kept bobbing her head or moving too quickly. After just a few minutes, she was tired and frustrated, so she stopped until the next day. With practice, she could keep the red laser dot on the green crosshairs almost perfectly.

It felt good to be able to do something right, and when she next met with her augmentation therapist, she appreciated being told that she was making progress. Cora went home and used the auglenses to start designing a game about her experience of recovering from surgery. The game blended images from the television shows and games she had played during her recovery, with the terrible daily news of the killings of Black and trans people by police and the images of people being teargassed by riot police for protesting the election. She turned it all into a story featuring a valiant interplanetary space guardian.

It was then that Cora's brother, Marcos, spoke to her. Cora was sitting on his couch, looking off into space and moving her head in unexplained ways, interacting with the virtual interface in her auglenses. He was sitting next to her, watching a streaming movie. "Hey, sis, can I talk to you?"

Cora blinked rapidly, then turned and looked at him, "Of course."

"Look, I can see that you're hurting, I mean, you've told me that you're hurting. I just want to offer something that may help but may seem crazy, so hear me out. Do you want to come to the gym with me? I don't think I've ever told you, but I feel like this gym saved my life. They have amazing programs there for gymnastics, boxing, and weightlifting."

"I don't want to do weightlifting," Cora said, "or anything that's going to make me look more masculine."

"I know, girl! But gymnastics?"

"Now that sounds awesome. And I've done a little boxing before," said Cora.

"Honestly, a year ago when I started lifting weights, I was depressed. I was afraid of being attacked on the street by homophobes. But learning to lift gave me so much confidence and courage. Now I know that my strength isn't just an idea, it is fucking real."

"Okay, I'll go with you once, but gyms have always been terrifying to me, honestly. As a kid, the gym was the place where I would get beat up. I figured out a way to get out of gym class by signing up for a VR design class at the same time and getting a special waiver," she said. "I would never feel safe enough to go by myself. But yes! I'll try it!"

"YES! OMG, let's watch *Stick It*! Have you seen it? It's the *Bring It On* of gymnastics!"

I laughed at Cora, and teased, "Ok, but what about *But I'm a Cheerleader*? Did you and Marcos watch that too?"

Cora said, "Absolute classic—love it. I think we had both already seen it enough times already. Rea, I'm so grateful to you for listening to all of this. I hope I'm not oversharing."

I looked into her eyes. "Cora, I just want to know you, I'm so honored that you want to share this with me. I'll be honest, it's hard to hear how depressed you were. I hope you can tell me more about how you came out of it and became the confident, gorgeous woman you are today."

Cora squirmed and blushed at the compliment, but she did agree to tell me more about how she found her strength.

CHAPTER 6.

Cora resumed telling me about her past on our next date, in sweet, intimate conversation, on an old red couch at a coffee shop where we shared a late-night cup of tea.

Her first time going with Marcos to the gym, Cora was nervous, but since he was with her, she wasn't afraid. They walked into the gym, with its pounding techno music and its intense odors of plastic off-gas from the flooring and the weights, mixed with the smell of sweat. Crossing to the back of the long narrow gym, past the pull-up rig and the punching bags hanging in rows, Cora and Marcos met the gymnastics coach.

Five other people joined the class, and they began with introductions and some stretching. Cora struggled to keep her voice in a female range over the loud music.

That first day they worked on handstands and rope climbs. Cora had done neither before, except as a child. The coach had been in gymnastics classes for years as a young girl, a life Cora wished she had enjoyed. But she was now making up for that! Cora kicked up and into a graceful handstand against the wall, having practiced other fitness methods enough to have a sense of where her body was in space and how to use it.

All of those practices though, like running and boxing, she had done as an adult. As a kid in elementary and middle school, and especially in gym class, Cora had been in many fights, none of which she started. It was so confusing to her why the boys said she was gay when she wasn't, she liked girls so much she thought about them all the time! It turned out they were right—she was gay, but in a way they never would have expected.

Now Cora was learning gymnastics, moving on to handstand push-ups. Cora had never heard of these before! But on her first try, she was able to follow the coach's instructions: from the position against the wall, lower your head close to the pad, pull your knees down to bend your legs, then kick up and push up with your arms at the same time. She did it! The coach said she was a natural, which made Marcos smile hard, and Cora laughed under her breath. "Thanks," she said brightly. It felt so good to be able to do something right again.

Marcos and Cora kept going to that gym, but after a few weeks, that coach was fired, and the owner took over her classes. The gym owner was a totally stereotypical meathead, with almost no neck to speak of, which seemed to impair his ability to articulate directions clearly. His idea of a beginner class was just "do fewer reps," and he was unwelcoming to Cora and Marcos, gruff in a macho, homophobic way. But soon Cora began her new job on the other side of town, and found an apartment nearby in the Mount Washington area and a new gym. She was sad not to work out with her brother anymore, but she had asked some friends and the new gym she found was queer friendly.

Walking into Rainforest Fitness for the first time, Cora was relieved to see the large rainbow flags hanging from the ceiling. Now this was a very different gym. She signed up for the on-ramp class, a series for beginners that introduced all the basic movements for strength training in detail, taught by the gym's co-owner. Tommy was East Asian, an expert gymnast, and incredibly fit, both muscular and lithe. He could hold an amazing ice cream maker on the rings: hands on the rings, body parallel to the floor, impressive and inspiring. Yet Tommy wasn't at all cocky; he was articulate, had studied the body for years and was passionate about teaching. Cora's first class went over the details of planks and squats, like how to use your scapulas and what parts of the gluteus muscles to focus on when squatting.

Lifting a barbell in a deadlift for the first time, picking the weight up off the ground and bringing it to standing, Cora was exhilarated. She let her fear of looking muscular go, finding that becoming aware of her strength felt so good to her. The next class she lay on the floor alternating between what Tommy called hollow—on her back, legs lifted, arms overhead, abs on fire—and arch—on her stomach, legs lifted, arms lifted behind her, breathing fast and trembling. All the while, she tracked her biometrics and her timer in her auglenses. In that moment, she thought that she wanted this to be her life. Finally, she felt alive again. Finally, she found something that she wanted to do, besides watching television and eating frozen tamales.

Rainforest Fitness also had a trainer, Gabe, who was open about being a trans guy, and Cora began taking classes with him. He was kind and warm, often giving Cora tips on her form or how to stay safe, even when he wasn't coaching her class but just walking by. To her absolute surprise, Cora began to love going to the gym. She increased her membership and was soon coming in three, four, then five days a week. Being able to feel her body, to be in her body, and to feel it reach its limits and still push through, was an incredible joy. Day after day, she went to Rainforest Fitness, doing combinations of squats with weights, snatches with barbells over her head, bench presses, and sit-ups that would have been unbelievable to her previous self. Day after day, she lay on the padded floor of the gym, covered in sweat, breathing hard, feeling like she had never worked so intensely.

Before or after her job designing 3D VR models and games, she was in the gym. On the weekends, she was in the gym. Some days she took two classes a day. Gradually her body started to change, which was scary to her. She had gotten surgery to look more female, and now that she had, was she making a mistake doing all this work that would make her more muscular? Cora examined herself in the mirror many nights, wondering. She texted Gabe about her fears, and he texted back, "If you are worried about your muscles looking too big, just stop working out and they'll go away. You are doing awesome. You should be proud of every single little muscle because you've worked for them."

Her depression had largely lifted. After a few weeks of getting fit, Cora decided to stop dating for a long time and to focus instead on her health and self-care. She decided to stop drinking, too, and started eating healthy and joined a weekly support group for trans women at the LGBT Center. It had been months since her experience with Lily, and she was learning to love herself, and enjoy her solitude. Cora began to treasure her body and herself as she worked hard to take care of herself and become the woman she wanted to be.

Then, something even bigger happened. Walking from the gym to her car one night, alone and on a dark area of the street, Cora heard the voices of three men as they walked up behind her. She had an impulse then to turn on her auglenses to record what might happen, but she realized that she felt differently now. For so many years, Cora had been afraid for her safety every day. When Cora decided to transition at twenty-nine, she believed the rhetoric that she could liberate herself from the colonial shackles of the gender binary and started immediately wearing miniskirts.

It took her years to grow her hair out and get both electrolysis and laser hair removal on her face, and in the meantime, Cora experienced numerous violent encounters. Twice she was attacked and punched on the street, and she found herself on the receiving end of hateful language daily. As a result, she learned to look at the floor. Literally. She was so afraid of experiencing more violence that she held close to her girlfriend at the time, and was often afraid of going out without her. When she was alone in public, she avoided eye contact as much as possible. She would hold her urine for long periods to avoid public restrooms and developed the habit of looking over her shoulder any time she heard someone coming up behind her. She practiced nodding and gesturing to cashiers to avoid people hearing her voice. Cora had been afraid and had shrunk herself because of it, had learned so many ways to make herself invisible. Now, that had changed.

From the first day of lifting class, Tommy emphasized the importance of posture. "You can't put a hundred pounds on your shoulders, in the back rack position, if you can't stand up straight without weights," he said. He taught the class to practice good posture from the beginning: shoulders back, take a deep breath, tuck the pelvis forward to align the lower spine, turn the ab muscles on, then breathe out into a strong, relaxed, straight posture. Cora practiced standing up straight, eyes ahead. The coaches didn't know the healing that was happening over and over whenever they reminded her, "Eyes up!" It was a cue that Cora fused into the deep part of herself.

Now as she was walking alone to her car, *she didn't feel afraid*. She held her neck straight, her upper back and core active, her thighs burning from class, and she looked forward, not at the floor. Arriving at her car, the NFC wireless signal from her auglenses bio-authenticated her, and the car door unlocked. The words, "Hello, Cora. Workout time: 1:49:00. Next appointment: Tomorrow, 11 a.m. Discuss Prototypes," appeared on the windshield, in a heads-up display that only she could see.

She felt strong, and unafraid, for the first time in so long. At this realization, she sat in her car and wept with joy.

CHAPTER 7.

Learning so much of her story over the first weeks we were dating was intense. But Cora's vulnerability in opening up to me made me feel like maybe I could share with her the losses I'd had. And one day, I might be able to share even the quantum truth of how the universe was taking those people from me.

Slow. Learning to go slow, to move slowly, to let my feelings grow, was a profound challenge. After four dates, I decided Cora could come to my apartment, so when she asked to come over after our dinner out—pupusas at a local Salvadorian restaurant—I hesitated. I wanted to say yes so badly, even though I hadn't cleaned my place. I looked at her and said, "You can come over, but we're not having sex."

"OMG, Rea! I didn't say we were!" she said.

"I know, I know, but you know how queers are. I mean, I know how I used to be, but I'm not that person anymore. And, like we both agreed, I want to take things slowly," I said.

"Of course," said Cora, "I was there for that conversation, remember?"

We laughed softly together as we climbed into Cora's car. We drove to my apartment quietly, letting our food settle. I looked out of the window; the speeding highway lights and neon signs on businesses in LA scrolling across my face and the car window. I thought of the millions of photons in our current reality, dancing in waves and particles simultaneously, giving us this moment in a process that was all such a mystery. The reds and yellows, the massive LED images of women's faces scrolling down the side of the Intercontinental Hotel, were soothing to me and so beautiful.

"And my place is a mess! But you can come for a little bit and have tea," I said. I decided it was a good milestone as we were becoming closer, and I was beginning to trust her a bit. I had my usual story ready about my hobby in physics.

We walked into my apartment, my dog barking at the presence of a stranger. Cora took a few steps in and stood in awe, taking in the longest wall of my place, on which I had painted in large characters, a couple feet tall and a few feet wide:

$$\mu i \equiv \langle \Psi_{UNIVERSE} \mid Pi \mid \Psi_{UNIVERSE} \rangle$$

On the other walls, I had sheets of butcher paper taped up, with my scribbled attempts at working through the many worlds interpretation. Sweeping lines of derivatives and integration symbols, Greek letters, and stars, lines of my attempts at solving the equations covered my walls instead of art. Piles of books were stacked in the corners, on the table, next to my couch, *on* the couch, many of them open, pens nearby, and lines underlined. Cora looked around the room, astonished. I plugged in the Christmas lights that dangled messily around the room, lighting the equations in a way that made them seem endearing, I hoped, instead of mad.

"I was never much of an interior designer, I have to confess," I said.

"Whoa, I thought you said you were a writer," said Cora.

I didn't hesitate with my routine answer. "Yeah, I am a poet and a dancer, but I love physics, so I study it as a hobby. It informs a lot of my work. I'm not alone; there are some amazing cultural theorists writing about quantum physics today," I said, as I moved to the pile of books on the table. I picked up

Michelle M. Wright's *Physics of Blackness* and Karen Barard's *Meeting the Universe Halfway.* "These are both amazing books that bring together race, gender, and quantum physics. These are more about matter and light, but my own interest is in the many worlds interpretation or MWI . . . "

Cora was still open mouthed and looking more closely at some of my equations. She said, "I thought I was the geek in this situation. I mean, I can code, but I don't know what these equations mean."

"That one is the square modulus of the wave function, which represents the probability distribution of finding the particle at position x," I said.

"Right . . . ," said Cora. Then she finally looked at me and smiled in a way that glowed with attraction. "I am so hot for your brain right now," she said.

"Tea!" I said, "Let's have tea, and you can tell me more about your own geeky loves."

"So, your hobby is that you want to understand the MWI?" Cora asked distractedly, not moving or responding to my offer for tea. She was looking at one of the equations with a glaze to her eyes, no doubt recording it with her auglenses.

"No, my hobby is I want to prove my own idea about the MWI. It follows, in my own gedankenexperiment—or thought experiment—that if one world splits off into another world as its timeline moves forward, then there must be an identifiable point where and when that split occurs. Given that, that point is identifiable, and implies that there is a possibility that one could somehow cross that point and move into the original world, move across realities, move across probability splits. My concern is that this may imply traveling in time, which might be impossible, but I am trying to prove that it does *not* require a negative movement across the time axis and so might therefore be possible."

Now Cora looked at me. She had heard me. She was no longer distracted or trying to be sexy. She looked at me with the seriousness of one mind meeting another to try to find new truths.

"That is quite a hobby, Rea." After a beat, she looked back at the same equation, closely, now lifting her hand and moving her outstretched fingers.

"What are you doing?" I asked.

"These are amazing," she said in awe. "My augs have a simple visualization tool that is showing me models of some of these equations, but it can't calculate some of them or the transformations between the steps of these proofs."

"But could they?" I asked, perking up optimistically.

Cora looked at me again, once more smiling seductively. She could tell that she had something I really wanted, and that seemed to bring her pleasure. She said, "I'm a 3D designer and coder. Creating these models is pretty similar to what I do for a living, but never with ideas as exciting as this. Anything can happen . . . "

Looking into her smiling eyes, I paused, my mouth slightly open, starting to say something but not saying anything. I definitely didn't want to use or manipulate her. I was developing feelings for her after learning so much about her, and now she was offering to help me with something so important to me, a way to understand myself, my past, and why I keep slipping through realities. I wanted to take things slow. I didn't want to risk losing her. But she was so close to my face now that I really wanted to kiss her.

"*Tea!*" I practically screamed and stepped away to the kitchen, leaving Cora to look at my equations. From the kitchen I called, "What kind do you want? Herbal, black, or ginger? I have some sweet rose tulsi, too!"

We sat on my couch that night, sipping sweet rose tulsi tea and talking largely about physics. I told Cora the story of Einstein and Bohr's disagreements over quantum physics and how their findings eventually led to the MWI. She smiled glowingly at our intellectual connection. The soft light was perfect for our cozy evening at opposite ends of my couch. My dog, Azul, sat patiently and watched us talking, her head resting between her front paws, waiting for her evening walk. She moved her eyes to look back and forth at the two of us as we gestured to equations or tried to depict the cosmos with our hands.

A few days later, Cora and I had another date in the middle of the week, on Tuesday. Cora came to my place again, and this time I'd had a chance to clean up. I vacuumed up all the dog hair, put some of the piles of books on the shelves, and took down some of my butcher paper full of proofs of equations about particle probabilities. Cora offered to cook me arepas, a Colombian specialty. As my family was Mexican, it was a treat.

My parents, Leonora and Jorge, lived in Mexico City, which they always called DF for Distrito Federal, before migrating to Los Angeles. They settled in Boyle Heights, a historically Chicano neighborhood, and felt at home in the sprawling mix of urban and suburban areas in LA. While not as byzantine and dense as DF, LA's sheer size provided them a similar feeling of being held by a community with a rich culture. They loved their neighbors, Tongva people and East Asian people from nearby Japan Town. On Saturdays, they enjoyed the incredible tamales and ingredients you could get in Mariachi Plaza, and the many communities of Latin American immigrants—Mexican, Colombian, Salvadorian, Cuban—made them feel quickly at home.

Cora loved arepas, corn flour patties fried on the stove and typically stuffed with cotija cheese and carne asada. But as she was really working on eating healthy to maintain her lean muscle, she wasn't having cheese tonight, so I wasn't either. She came over and began cooking immediately, very comfortable in the kitchen. She pulled all the ingredients out of her canvas bag: the masa flour, a lime, flank steak, butter, and fresh salsa. First, she set the meat in a bowl to marinate, then washed her hands and moved on to creating the dough.

I often struggled to cook for myself, so this was a delight. Watching Cora measure out the masa flour and the water, I felt such affection for her. She was showing me that, now that we had been dating for a few weeks, she wanted to do something generous and caring for me. I stood in the door of the kitchen looking at her with warmth in my eyes. Cora mixed the masa, butter, salt, and water together in the bowl. She told me that her mother had made arepas when she was little but never taught her how to cook them. Cora didn't learn until she was an adult how to really cook for herself. She had read recipes for arepas online and tried a few variations in cooking times and ingredient proportions until she found the combination that made delicious arepas that were crispy on the outside and fluffy on the inside.

Eating arepas spoke to something deep in Cora—perhaps genetic memory, perhaps the childhood trauma of growing up separated from her father in prison and her parents' divorce that both made her feel distant from her Colombian heritage. Arepas con queso y carne were one of the few small ties that Cora felt to the faraway place her father was from.

Cora explained all this as she kneaded the dough. She wanted to share a deep part of herself with me. I moved closer to her. I felt closer to her. She looked up from her focused kneading, and I was standing right next to her, leaning on the kitchen counter, and kissed her. Our lips met and then our tongues met. She stopped kneading, her hands resting in the wet dough as we kissed. Our deep longing, a deep sense of shared history, shared pain, and shared joy made itself felt in that kiss. The kiss was long and powerful. Pulling away from her, I looked at her, and we both smiled.

"Wow," said Cora breathily. I laughed a little and walked away so she could finish cooking our dinner.

CHAPTER 8.

I wasn't being totally honest with Cora, but I was afraid to tell her the truth. If I told her what I had experienced, she would think I was crazy. Maybe I was crazy—could it be real? If I told her the truth, she would close off from me emotionally. The truth was too hard to tell her: that if we had a moment of intense, passionate connection, I might disappear, she might disappear, our entire relationship timeline might disappear in a quantum reaction of probabilities that starts with a chemical reaction in my neurochemistry. I couldn't tell her. But I could tell her that I had a theory I was working on and ask her to help me. Ugh. It became messy so quickly, but if she could actually help me find the cause or a way to change it, maybe things could be different with Cora.

The sun was setting in a blaze of orange outside of my window when Cora rang the buzzer to come up to my apartment for our next date. Azul started barking excitedly and defensively, and I shooshed her as I ran to the mirror to double check my hair before Cora reached my door. I wondered if she already thought I was crazy, with my equations scrawled on butcher paper covering the walls of my apartment, and wondered, too, if she would really be able to help with such a complex problem. The late sunlight beamed onto one side of the apartment, lighting up half of my work with a brightness that gave me hope for a moment. She knocked, I opened the door, and she came in and kissed me. Azul barked, but I didn't interrupt that excited, beautiful kiss to quiet her. She quieted herself a few moments later, perhaps picking up on how much I was melting into Cora's lips.

She had brought her laptop along. Wirelessly connecting to my projector allowed her to show me all the layers of images her auglenses produced.

"Okay Rea, where do we start?" Cora asked, looking around the room, resting her eyes on different equations. When her auglenses recognized symbols like $\int$, the integral symbol, it would highlight the equation, calculate what it could, and display an animated graph of the result. As Cora passed her gaze across the various calculations, the images on screen morphed into different shapes, curved lines, parabolas—a plane that looked like paper, bent into different combinations of curves and folds.

I made my way to an equation on the opposite wall. "We're going to have to focus here, on the moment of probability selection and waveform collapse. I want to be able to dig into that moment to see how it can be affected by the other quantum chemical states around it."

Cora turned to look at the set of equations I was pointing to, and the screen went blank. "Okay," she said, "I'm going to have to do some coding to get these models to work together."

We worked together for a few hours that night, ordering Thai food so we could keep going. I broke down the equations into smaller and smaller steps, until Cora's algorithms could find models for them, then she worked on translating the logic between the steps into visual forms. I felt connected to her in a new way, then, sharing an intellectual challenge, admiring her abilities and showing her mine. It was a rare form of connection, and it was compounded by the attraction and affection I already felt for her. It was also a good way to keep us busy but still together, keeping my mind off sex (for the most part), helping me to wait, and letting our relationship develop. This was a foreign feeling to me. I was struggling to grow new mental and emotional habits in hopes that this time could be different.

We had more dates like that one. Over the next month, we kept working on modeling the equations of quantum probability theory across many worlds. Often, we ended those nights watching a film together or cuddling on my couch—but I kept my bedroom off limits. Cuddling and making out was already so tempting. Azul nearly burst with excitement whenever Cora arrived, who was always ready to sit on the floor with her and get covered in Azul's white fur, even let her lick her face. Yuck.

We also had regular dates when we were not working at my apartment. We walked through the park together with Azul. I loved sharing with Cora the beauty I saw in the curving complexity of the trees. We watched the sunset many times over the expanse of water below the park. Cora's face was so beautiful in that light. As I shared more of myself with her, I knew that I wanted to tell her the truth about my experience and my so-called physics hobby. As a hacker herself, she didn't question my intellectual passion for physics and the joy that made me leap up with my arms in the air at every small advance we made, when her visual models helped us get one small step farther in solving the equations we were working on. After one success like that, I hugged her so hard, she laughed, and I cried a little bit over her shoulder, feeling more and more intensely that I did not want to lose her. I deeply hoped our work would be successful.

One evening at dusk, we watched the sparkling of the lights from the homes across the water in Malibu Beach turning on. I thought of the quantum effects that created that illusion of sparkle, allowing some photons to reach our eyes and not others, and how that sparkle must even now be working at a different oscillation in Cora's eyes. Watching her eyes as she looked into the distance, I decided I would tell her the truth about my past, soon.

There were major challenges to our efforts. One particularly hard-to-code model of a probability wave function seemed to have Cora beaten. The night we started working on it, I described the equations to her, and she came up with a simple visualization, and showed it to me. But I told her it was not enough. She said she'd combine them and add more detail to one of the variables that controlled the spinning momentum. She worked and worked on that for hours. Meanwhile, I worked on other parts of the equation but eventually ran out of steam. She told me she wanted to keep working, and I turned my attention to a film and relaxed.

Later, Cora told me how she finally solved the problem. Coding was something that happened for Cora both consciously and unconsciously. It definitely required many hours of sitting in front of her keyboard, debugging, trying different approaches to a problem, running them, visualizing them, and then going back, iterating the code in a different way, and executing it. But she also said that many of her best ideas came when her conscious mind was occupied with something else, when she was tinkering away in the back of her mind on the problem.

One morning she was up early at Rainforest Fitness. Her workout started with a run while it was still dark, with a rare LA rain, just a light rain, and a thin mist. She ran with the group of five in her class. She put up her black hood against the rain and thought about how running had just become such an important skill to work on. The new president had been elected on a platform that was vehemently anti-gay, anti-trans, and anti-immigrant, and Cora felt her Latina heritage more strongly now that she was likely to be targeted for it.

For years, she had carried with her the fear of being a trans Latina woman, one of the groups most targeted for violence and murder. Now her fears were amplified daily by videos broadcast on the internet of the new president calling for more deportations, more walls, and for the stripping away of legal protections for trans people. Within days of taking office, he had begun to revoke civil liberties for trans people, including the right to see a doctor and the right to even enter businesses that did not want trans people there. The threat of compulsory electroshock treatments for LGBT people was also broadcast widely; it was here, and it was real. As groups like the ACLU promised to fight these measures, the new administration made vague claims of jailing all gay people. Additionally, they seemed to have a clear vision of profit—and of enforcing a new social order—from building more prisons for Muslim people, immigrants, queer and trans people.

While some were surprised by how fast hateful campaign promises were kept and by the brisk realities of police tracking down families and knocking down doors, Cora, for her part, was getting ready. She lifted her gaze to the horizon, tightened her core, and focused on pushing her legs behind her, harder, faster. Running, she thought, could save her life.

Finishing her run and panting hard, she along with the rest of the group poured back into the gym. Up next were snatches, her favorite. Cora had only learned Olympic lifting in the past year of being at Rainforest, but already she loved it. The snatch was one of the most technical moves—taking the barbell off the ground and overhead in a single, fast motion by pulling hard and lifting as high as possible with the shoulders and feet. For a split millisecond, she was off the ground and using that momentum to get the weight directly overhead as she squatted as low as possible to the ground, in one continuous movement. The move finished with her standing up straight, the weight still overhead and holding it still, before dropping it to the ground.

Cora practiced her snatch over and over, gradually lifting a few kilograms at a time to her max of forty-five kilograms. Sweat dripping from her brow, her eyes focused hard on the ground in front of her. Then she shifted her gaze up to the cinder block wall across the gym as she lifted the weight again and again. Her tattooed arms were working their hardest, shaking as she reached her maximum weight and tried to hold it over her head.

Each time she swung the weight up from the ground, in the back of her mind she thought about the momentum of particles, electrons, subparticles, gluons, and their spin, their probability to jump from one state to another. As the bravado of the rapper in the hip-hop song pounded around her and the others in her class lifted their weights in kind, unconsciously, she considered how to code the model of the moment when one universe of probability splits off into another. Her conscious mind focused on turning on her lats, raising up to relevé with her feet, squatting low, getting under the weight, while the repetitive part of her mind that wouldn't give up kept turning over the problem in the code.

Dropping the weight with the loud clang of metal plates slapping together, she realized what was missing: data! If she could just find research data on quantum entanglement in photons at the moment of wave collapse, the moment of probability selection, she could finish the model that Rea needed! When she announced this to her lifting partner, she looked at her as if those words were far crazier than trying to lift an incredibly heavy weight over your head in a single movement.

With the rush that came with her breakthrough, she told her coach she was done for the day, packed up, and practically ran to my apartment. She texted me on the way to make sure I'd be home for a work/play date, typing and smiling and speed walking down the sidewalk to her car. When I opened the door, she had that smile on again, the one that indicated she understood that her brilliance was sexy to me, that she had figured out another part of the puzzle we had been working on for months now, and that she knew I would be grateful, would definitely show her just how grateful I was. Our connection had grown so much by spending time together but also by building something beautiful and complex together, our 3D model of the equation. I knew I had to tell her soon about my unfortunate and bizarre ability over which I had no control.

"Data!" she said, her eyes widening and still smiling. She stood in the doorway. "If we can just find some data on quantum entanglement of photons at the moment of wave collapse, I can add that to our probability matrix, and we can finish the model! We just need to run a large-scale analysis on the data about observer m, the one whose presence causes the probabilities to be determined!"

At that, my heart sank, and my smile softened with a tinge of sadness, "Aw, babe, it's really sweet that you're so excited, but I've been down that road before. Come in, I made pollo a la criolla!"

"What!" she exclaimed, as she came in and set her bag down. Azul bounced on her back paws for attention and Cora bent down to pet her, but Azul kept evading her and licking her hand instead. "I *love* criolla! My mom used to make that!"

I angled my head and put my hands on my hips. "I know that. Why do you think I made it for us?!"

As we sat enjoying the rich flavor of cumin and tomato, perfectly runny egg yolk dripping onto the chicken and avocado, I told her why I wasn't as excited at her discovery. "That data exists, babe, but it's not public. It's part of the Army's ghost imaging program."

Cora paused for a moment, her fork held above her food, her eyes resting on me. "The Army?" she said. "But isn't physics research published so that other researchers can verify and improve on it? Isn't that how academics work?"

"Yeah," I said, "that's how academics work. But you know there is a ton of research being done by non-academics. I've been following the work of guys like Ronald E. Masers and TJ Rovindan, and these guys are working on similar questions to what we're doing but for very different ends."

She kept eating and between bites said, "You mean for murder kind of ends?"

"Of course, that's the end. But their stated goal is ghost imaging: using quantum entanglement to be able to image objects before the light hits the object, being able to image targets their sensors can't see."

Cora's expression hardened from the joy of eating pollo a la criolla to one more serious and caused me some concern. "Well, if they have the data, and that's what we need," she said, "I'll get us the data."

My feelings for Cora were strong enough by now that those words generated a deep fear in me. It was a familiar old feeling in my chest, just to the right of center, like stillness or emptiness. That fear was almost as old as I was, the fear of losing someone I love—losing my father first when he left us, then my mother to her mental illness, then slipping so many times and losing lovers, partners, friends. My chest was a knot of two feelings, the terror of losing Cora to prison and the intense desire to discover how to keep myself from slipping into another universe where she no longer exists. Finally, after a short moment full of so many emotions for me, I spoke.

"You can't," I said. "It's not worth it. We can find another way."

Cora's brow furrowed; she could see the emotional waves crossing my body. "We've been trying to solve this problem with math alone, but neither of us have the skill for that. We can keep working on this for years, but you talk about this as if it is urgent. We can solve this problem from another angle, filling the curve with data instead of grasping for the perfect equation for that curve. But you have to tell me what this is all about, Rea. I see you. I care about you. I feel your fear right now, and I've felt your intense need to solve this as quickly as possible. You think you've been playing it cool, I guess, but I know you have something more to tell me."

My fear deepened into my stomach, and I felt the slowing of time that comes with the rush of neurochemicals in a fight or flight response. Fuck. I was so afraid of losing her, and now

I had to tell her something that was probably going to make her leave. Well, it had only been a few months; maybe I could get over her. I looked down at the meal I had lovingly made for us, afraid that it might be our last together, and began to cry.

"Babe, it's okay. I'm sorry!" She put her hand on my knee. "I don't want to upset you. I just need to know why this hobby of yours is so important to you. Especially if I'm going to go back to my old ways of getting into dot mil servers for you."

I looked at her through blurry vision, my face red and hot from crying, tears dripping off my cheeks, as those last words sunk in. She was willing to risk her freedom because she could tell how important this was to me. It wasn't going to make much sense, but I had to be honest with her, finally. I decided to let the conscious part of my mind move forward with honesty, which I knew was the right thing to do, even though my body was screaming at me to stop.

"I have a problem. I didn't want to tell you. You're not—it's hard to believe. Maybe I'm crazy," I stopped and cried some more, wiping my mouth and nose sloppily with a napkin.

"Well, *I'm* definitely crazy, so that is not a problem for me, hun," Cora said, looking at me compassionately, a slight smile lifting one side of her mouth.

"No, but seriously. And you are not fucking crazy. You are brilliant and strong and powerful, and maybe people see that as crazy, but I see it as you choosing who you are and creating yourself. Okay, I'm going to tell you as much as I've been able to figure out. Fuck it! If you want to leave after I've told you this, I won't hold it against you or be surprised."

Cora started to protest, and I held my palm toward her, "Please, just listen first." I regained some of my composure as I accessed the story I had been preparing for weeks to tell her. "For years now, I've had this problem. I slip. At first, I thought I was losing my mind. One moment I was with this woman having incredible, passionate, tender sex, and the next she was gone. I was alone. It felt like I had dreamed it and suddenly woken up, but that didn't make any sense. I was naked in bed, but I was wide awake."

Cora watched me with a combination of affection, fear, and concern. I felt she was afraid of the words coming out of my mouth for the same reason I was: because she knew she might have to leave depending on what was said. As I spoke, her expression changed slightly to one of curiosity. I could almost see the equations tumbling around in her head as she began to grasp that my problem spanned realities.

CHAPTER 9.

13:00:45 <@nepantla> still looking for a waterwitch.
need to cast a finding spell

13:01:30 <@quimera> have you tried asking en los
canales patriarcados?

13:01:31 <@quimera> the patriarchal channels??

13:42:49 @nepantla (+i) Away. 2:#akellare_cyborg (+Cnt)

The light of the characters—neon green against a dark background—flickered as the text chat scrolled upward. By can-
dlelight, in near darkness, Luz sat cross-legged in meditation,
eyes closed, hands folded in her lap. Her long curly brown
hair lay across the black scarf draped across her shoulders.
She often thought the scarf, thin but woven of thick thread
with frayed edges, looked like a mourning garment. But more
importantly: it looked witchy.

Luz inhaled deeply, stretching her spine upward as she envisioned connecting to the stars and galaxies far above her head. Then she sent her attention rushing down through her body, and through the earth. She pictured in her mind the arms of the trees she walked among at night along with her black dog, the way they moved slightly with the cold wind, the bright moonlight through them. Trees are the goddess incarnate, hundreds of years of strength and energy flowing through them. She was preparing to ask the goddess to help her find the hacking hardware that she needed to locate her mother.

Luz was sharing an apartment with her friend Gloria. For years, she had moved from place to place, finding a home wherever she could. She had been told that her mother had given her away to a friend's family when she was just two years old. And then her mother disappeared. Luz had no memories of her after that point.

She had moved so many times as a child that she couldn't even count the number of places she'd lived. When she was thirteen, she had been able to live with a friend, Luisa, and her friend's mother, Connie, for a few years. She grew to think of them as family. One night after school, Luz waited for hours to be picked up by Connie. No one came. Finally, she called Gloria, Connie's older daughter, and asked for a ride. Gloria was eighteen at that point, and attending college to study psychology. Driving home from the school, they sat in silence. Luz watched the stripes of light and dark moving across her arm and the car's interior. Finally, Gloria began to speak in low, sad tones.

She said, "My mom was admitted to a psychiatric hospital. She has schizophrenia. We don't know when she will be out." Her own devastation was clear in her voice. "I'm sorry, but you're going to have to move again. The plan is for you to go live with my dad—Connie's ex-husband. His name is Jesus."

Luz kept watching the moving lines of black shadow and cold blue streetlight moving rapidly inside the car. She turned away from Gloria as the tears streamed down her face, as it involuntarily wrinkled, and she sobbed. She didn't grasp the full meaning of Gloria's words, but she knew she was losing Connie, losing someone who had mothered her, someone who had been kind to her. Jesus had visited occasionally and provided Connie some financial support in raising Luz, but she didn't know him at all. She had no idea of what living with him might be like.

Jesus Herrera was named by his pious parents. And he inherited their piety not just in name but also in spirit. He learned from his grandfather to be a god-fearing man, to share his faith loudly and publicly, to keep a statuette of baby Jesus on the dashboard, and to teach his children religion. Jesus learned to go to church on Sunday and wait until Monday to beat his wife. Luz moved into his home with his entire family, his wife and two children. They were instantly unwelcoming. Their discomfort at having this new weird kid in their house was palpable. Jesus had a son, Mauro, who was two years older than Luz, and a daughter, Maria, who was three years younger. Jesus made Luz share a room with Mauro; it was a small room that was a makeshift addition to the garage, with a bunk bed inside.

Mauro's favorite hobbies were working out, cleaning his sneakers, making sure his hair stayed perfectly combed, and playing cruel tricks on the girls he brought home after school. One day as Luz was reading the book *Wild Seed* by Octavia Butler, Mauro came in through the back sliding door of the house with a girl. They were obviously here to have sex, but first Mauro told the girl to sit in the living room and offered her a glass of water. The girl sat on the couch, her back to Luz. Luz, meanwhile, was sitting at the kitchen counter, reading, facing the sink.

Mauro came over and poured some water into a glass, then put just a drop of dish soap in it, looking at Luz and winking with a smile. Luz, wanting nothing to do with this scene, frowned at him and resumed her reading. The girl drank a few sips from her glass and asked why the water tasted like soap. Mauro put on his best act of having no idea what could be wrong with the it. She had a few more sips, then said, "No, really, you should taste it. Something's wrong with this."

Mauro just replied, "No, baby, I'm sure it's fine."

He got up, took the glass, and made it look like he was tasting it as he walked to the kitchen and poured it out.

"Let's go," he said, gesturing with his head to the bedroom and smiling. Apparently, he had gotten enough arousal out of torturing the young girl and was ready to move on. She followed him into the bedroom. Mauro's sense of ethics was deeply warped by the situation he was living in.

Some nights, Luz could hear Jesus upstairs arguing violently with his wife, Sol. One terrifying night, Luz sat in her bed trying to read *The Dispossessed* while the pounding of footsteps shook the roof over her head. Her Español wasn't yet good enough to make out the cruel words being screamed, which was a gift for Luz. The next morning, leaving for school, she saw Sol at the top of the stairs, her face bruised, her arm tucked in a makeshift sling. Luz paused and looked at her, mirroring the pain on her face. This was a rare moment of connection. So many times, Sol had stood at the top of those stairs and screamed at Luz for not cleaning enough, or for not coming home on time, or for leaving a square of toilet paper hanging from the roll. Now, she said nothing as Luz walked out of the front door on her way to her first-period class.

It was in this environment that Luz first began to meditate. She had heard Gloria mention that meditation was a growing part of her life, an increasingly important spiritual practice. So, Luz checked some books on meditation out of the school library. It was her favorite place to be, and she often stayed in the library until it closed. Sol had been furious so many times at Luz's coming home so late. She couldn't believe that a young child could want to spend so many hours at the library.

Sol would yell, "Where have you been? I've been worried sick about you, carajo!"

To which Luz would reply, "I told you, I was at the library. They have a computer lab. I was learning BASIC! You can call them tomorrow and ask!"

But Sol never actually cared enough to follow up. She only cared enough to let her rage out on Luz, since she couldn't let it out on Jesus. If Sol had called, she would've learned from the staff that Luz was actually spending all of her time checking out books and learning to code. She was typing in lines like

10 PRINT "I LOVE TANIA"

20 GOTO 10

to create a program that would repeat, forever, the words "I LOVE TANIA." She thought this might impress girls. Luz was also learning more advanced programming techniques, but none of these skills seemed to impress any of the girls she wanted to date.

Living with Jesus and his family was intolerable, so Luz turned inwards. She tried to escape by spending as much time as she could reading. When she learned about meditation, she decided to try it. She shared a walk-in closet with Mauro that was small, like their room, both being created from divisions installed into the garage. But it provided some small amount of privacy. In that closet with its fluorescent light, Luz read about counting her breaths, bringing her attention to her breath, sitting in full lotus position. She put the book down at her side and tried what she had read, finding a tiny moment of peace, breathing in, breathing out.

She continued to find more books on meditation, which led her to books about the occult and witchcraft. When she read about worship of a female goddess embodied in nature, she felt an instant, deep connection. Connie had always made her go to Catholic church, even though her prayers for money never seemed to help out their family. Jesus also forced her to go to church, and Luz came to understand the masculinity of the Son of God to be the same kind of cruelty she saw in her caretaker, Jesus, who had assumed the role of her father and all the violence he understood in that kind of authority. As much as living with Jesus was intolerable to Luz, she could now see that she had been intolerable to him, because of the way she rejected masculinity completely.

When she turned fourteen and started high school, Luz joined an afterschool theater program for students with high IQ's called Mind Odyssey. Any time she could get out of the house and escape the violence, she would. Jesus' singular ethical quality was that he insisted Luz go to college, so he agreed to her joining the program, since he thought this might help her applications. Maybe it was just a way to get her out of his house, but Luz wanted to understand his commitment to her education as an act of care.

Mind Odyssey was a combination of theater and robotics, where students would work in teams on challenges for competitions. Luz loved everything about this program, but she particularly loved being able to perform as a character named Tulia. Luz volunteered to play Tulia, even though many other kids in her school would look at her and say that she wasn't a girl. Somehow, it just made sense to her, in her body and in her emotions. By now, Luz had grown her hair out long and curly, and Jesus hadn't tried to stop her. After a few months of wearing them on stage, Luz realized that she loved lipstick and tights and began to wear them every day.

Jesus's entire goal in Luz's upbringing was to ensure she understood that she had to be the breadwinner, that she had to learn to be a man. Every time these words came out of his mouth, she felt deeply how ridiculous it was. Even with her young understanding of herself, her body, and gender, Luz knew that Jesus's rigid concept of being a man wasn't based in any reality that Luz could relate to.

It wasn't long after Luz's realization of the joy her girl body brought her that the violence intensified in many ways. One afternoon, Luz and her friends in Mind Odyssey were waiting for the theater to be opened, to get to work on the second act of their electronic musical theater show. Luz leaned against a wall, looking down reading a book, when a group of boys walked past.

She had seen them coming, had encounters with them in the past, and she knew they looked for opportunities to inflict more violence on her. So, she tried to not be noticed. The four boys were caught up in their conversation, laughing about something else, until the moment when the last of them passed in front of Luz and punched her straight in the chest. Against the wall already, the impact instantly knocked the wind out of her. She dropped the book, coughing hard. Her friends just stood by in fear, pulling away to avoid being hit as well. The group of boys exploded with even louder laughter and kept walking. Their point was made—Luz wasn't even worth a fight.

Just days later, Luz stood in the kitchen making a sandwich, just home from school. Mauro came in the back door, threw his backpack down on a chair, and pushed her out of his way to get to the fridge. Luz screamed at him.

"What the fuck, man?!"

"What you gonna do, pussy?" he said through tight clenched teeth, putting his face inches from hers.

Luz was furious. And she was so confused. She had no outlets for her anger. Her rage twisted inside her, at her new stepmother, at her new father, at the boys who chased her home after school on so many afternoons. And now all that rage finally had a target in Mauro. He had been cruel and threatening to her so many times over the last two years, but now that she was openly wearing lipstick and a skirt, she feared his threats to beat the shit out of her were about to become real. Luz grabbed the large, sharp knife she had been using to cut the meat and cheese she was preparing to eat, stepped back, and pointed it at Mauro, holding it tensely between them.

"Get the fuck away from me," she yelled, barely able to get words out.

Incredibly, Jesus still did not kick her out after that. Maybe violence was so normalized to him that he wasn't disturbed by what had happened. Or maybe Mauro never told him. Regardless, Luz came to her own conclusions. Based largely on the fantasies she had read in books by Anaïs Nin and Henry Miller, she had decided she would run away to either New York or Paris.

Luz sat down next to Jesus one night as he and Sol sat drinking and playing poker. She was afraid. She had seen Jesus be violent so many times, but amazingly, he had never hit her.

Maybe it was because she was in the guidance counselor's office at school so often. Maybe it was her new meditation practice. Maybe it was the small black tourmaline she held in her hands to ground her as she did it. But she said to Jesus, "I can't live here anymore. I'm either going to run away, and you'll never see me again, or if you still want to help me, you can find me somewhere else to live."

She was shocked when Jesus, without missing a beat, answered, "You can go live with Gloria. I'll help you."

It was an incredible gift from the goddess.

And seemed too good to be true. Luz only said, "Thank you," and went back to her room.

At the time, she'd thought that Jesus did have a bit of kindness in him after all. Yet reflecting on it now, now that Luz fully understood herself to be a girl, she could see that it must have been his revulsion, his desire to get rid of her as much as if not more than any kindness.

Months later, Gloria came running up the stairs to their shared apartment, carrying a box. She was joyously calling Luz's name, "Luz! LUZ! I GOT IT!"

"You got what?!" said Luz, confused.

"I got you a PowerMac 6100!"

"WHAT?!" Luz screamed, "HOW?!"

"It *fell off the truck*, if ya know what I mean, at work," she said, with a sly grin.

Luz couldn't even believe her luck. Not only was she living with someone she had come to think of like a sister, and she could do pretty much whatever she wanted, despite being only sixteen, and now she had her own powerful computer! Gloria kindly gave Luz her space and respected her autonomy. It was a perfect arrangement for her, because Luz had a new girlfriend.

Much of Luz's time was now spent making out in her girlfriend's green vintage MG sports car, learning more about witchcraft, and studying hacking. Now that she had her own computer, she spent a lot of time online. She had quickly learned how to break into the local university's computer system. After getting in through a service left open on a rarely used port, Luz swiped a copy of the password file and used a dictionary tool to crack a handful of accounts easily.

With those accounts in hand, some of which had been used only once by students who had created and then forgotten them, Luz was able to gather more accounts on more important servers beyond the university network. She did this by trading with other hackers in IRC chatrooms but also by using the accounts she already had to break into other servers in other cities and countries. After learning BASIC when she was younger, she had moved on to learning C, which had enabled her spot and understand flaws in the code for Linux, the operating system that powered many servers.

While waiting for a program to crack the encryption on her newest batch of login/password combinations that she had swiped from a poorly maintained web server, she would read about witchcraft. Luz learned to cast circles of protection, to scry visions in flames, and to use tarot for divination. She learned to call on the spirits of the air, water, earth, and fire to aid and protect her in her excursions across the net. She had seen the ways that the feds had come down on other hackers, but she was driven.

Her biggest motivation was to find out the truth about her mother. Luz didn't know enough about her mother to find out exactly where she'd given birth to her. And as a minor, she didn't think they would give her any information anyway. She thought it couldn't have been too far from where Connie lived. So, now she was about to break into the computers of the hospital where she suspected she might have been born. It wasn't the most ethical choice, and maybe wasn't the most effective way to get the information, but she didn't have a lot of options, so she was using the skill she knew she could rely on: hacking.

CHAPTER 10.

The hack was so easy for Cora that she didn't even have to reach out to any friends for help. Because of her deep disapproval of the wars the US was engaged in, the Army's servers had been one of Cora's favorite targets at earlier times in her life. Aside from the respect this conferred on her by fellow hackers for having the skill to hack into dot mil servers, Cora felt ethically obligated to learn how to disrupt the workings of a racist imperialist regime, in any small ways she could.

After a brief Google search, this time she found her way in via the email addresses of the project's key researcher and one of his colleagues. She wrote a simple malware program and embedded it inside of a slide deck she made using a presentation program that generated an executable file. Yet she imagined that a military research physicist would never just open an unknown attachment, which was why she needed his colleague's address. Cora probed servers related to the lab on nearby domains until she found just what she needed: a mail server just slightly out of date.

There would only be a small window to use the exploit while it was unpatched, so she quickly opened a terminal window and used telnet to connect to the mail server's unencrypted port (port 25). Using the exploit program she had downloaded from the announcement of the security gap, Cora was able to create a fake email and spoof the sender address to appear as the colleague's. She then typed up a quick note asking the researcher to please review the attached presentation on the new sexual harassment policy.

Cora guessed it would be a document that he would not look at too closely, and she was able to find a copy of a similar policy document online. She made a few tiny changes and imported the slides into the program. The executable form of the slideshow it produced allowed Cora to use a decompiler and insert a small payload of malware that would be quietly copied onto the researcher's computer when the program was run. Cora finished uploading the attachment, finalized the email transmitting the SMTP protocol commands one by one into the terminal, and closed the port. Sitting in her bed, under the covers, she looked at the display and keyboard that only she could see in her auglenses. The low light from her burgundy lampshade illuminated the smile that spread across her face—she felt keenly the thrill of having used her skills for exactly what Rea needed. She felt that young part of herself that yearned for approval singing out in anticipation of Rea's pleasure.

Three days later, Cora was in her apartment reading news online about the horrifying acts of the new administration, now blocking immigrants from Muslim countries from entering its borders, even those who held legal green cards. Alternating waves of profound sadness, rage, and frustration hit her. But she was jerked out of the swirl of feelings by a small popup alert in her auglenses that faded into the edge of her vision. The alert simply read, "phoning home . . . "—something she had coded into her listener software. Cora jumped out of her seat, put both of her fists in the air, and screamed with joy. The small, unassuming alert signaled that the researcher had finally opened the fake attachment, and her malware program had been copied onto his hard drive.

The malware waited for a moment of idle time, when the researcher's computer was on but not directly being used. When a period of idle keyboard and mouse activity was detected, the malware then initiated a scan for the data files that Cora wanted. Once it found them, it opened a small, encrypted connection, using the Tor network to obscure Cora's IP address, and began to upload the files. When the upload was complete, the program deleted itself. In celebration, Cora danced around her apartment to the sound of FKA Twigs' deep bass and rapid electronic drum lines.

Over the months they had been together, Cora and Rea had grown closer, now that Cora knew the truth about Rea's history. Their bond intensified through sharing their stories, their hopes, and vulnerabilities, and now through their shared knowledge of this illegal hack. They both cared strongly for each other and knew they were at risk. When they met up for work dates—how they referred to their weekly time using the secret data stolen from the Army physics lab to construct their visual model—they shared determination and passion, and the sense of danger.

Cora reassured Rea that the hack had been pulled off perfectly, that the malware did its job, uploaded the files over an encrypted and onion-routed connection that was untraceable, and then deleted itself. She wanted Rea to love her so badly that she was willing to break the law for her, and maybe even enough to lie to herself for Rea. Cora knew that there was still some small chance that the hack could be detected, and no matter her assurances, Rea held that suspicion, too. Their disagreements about the possibility of being found out added tension to the fear they sometimes felt, which was however alleviated by their excitement whenever they made progress on the equations.

One morning as Cora was cooking breakfast, still in her underwear and a gray ripped t-shirt with a large skull and crossbones on it, Rea came into the kitchen in her robe and leaned against the doorframe.

She turned her gaze to the floor, "Babe, the reason I still worry about the hack is because I want to have a baby with you."

Cora looked at Rea, spatula in her left hand, eggs and soyrizo sizzling in the pan, smiled, blinked, and wrinkled her forehead at the wave of tenderness she felt for Rea.

"I know we haven't known each other very long, just over a year," Rea went on, looking up at Cora's expression and starting to cry in response, "but I want to be able to hold on to what we have, even if we get separated. No matter what separates us."

Cora felt the fear and the joy welling up so powerfully inside her that tears streamed down her face. She moved to Rea and hugged her as hard as she thought she could without hurting her.

Pulling back, still holding Rea, she said, "It's not going to be simple, you know. We'll have to contact the fertility clinic and find a friend who would carry a baby for us. And sign a lot of forms and get the timing right."

"I know it's never going to be an accident for us to have a kid, Cora, but I think we can make it happen," Rea said, smiling through her tears. "If we want to?"

"Of course, we want to! I mean—hell, I mean *I* want to! We need to talk about the finances, and we need to talk about apartments, and we—"

Rea kissed Cora deeply, holding her face in her hand, interrupting her list of practicalities even though she knew very well that Cora was right; she'd heard enough.

Smelling the eggs burning, Cora abruptly turned back and flipped them, causing them both to laugh hard.

Cora ran through her warm-up, hood up to protect from the cold dark morning air and the miasma of racism she felt swirling in the country. On her way to the gym, Cora had seen a notice from Metatext flash in her auglenses that Immigrations and Custom Enforcement (ICE) had started raids and checkpoints in Miami, the city where she'd grown up. She was so angry. And she knew that the raids and checkpoints were coming to LA any day now, too.

Not looking at her running partners, she gazed ahead and mostly at the ground as she brooded. She was worried about Rea, and she was worried for herself, that she might lose Rea. It was hard for Cora to sort out whether she thought Rea was losing her mind, or if she was telling the truth and she really was some superpowered quantum traveler with no control over her abilities. When she thought it out, Cora felt more like she was the one losing her mind for believing Rea's story.

She finished her run and headed down the ramp into the gym. Rainforest Fitness was basically a basement, cinder block walls covered up with planks of wood for doing handstands and wallballs. Cora loved it. It made her feel tough, training in this place with steel bars and exposed walls, though she didn't know if the owners were intentional about the aesthetic or if they were just saving money. She pulled out her barbell, added the weights to it with the telltale sound of the slide, then the loud slam of the plates against each other, and started her cleans, furiously lifting the bar from the floor. Focusing on holding her core solidly helped her take her mind off everything else, but in the back of her consciousness Cora was still wrestling with the question of Rea and her reality.

She did not want to lose Rea; she would do anything to keep her. Cora added two more metal plates to the bar. She squatted down, grasped the bar, and pulled it off the ground with all her strength, lifting it in one motion up to the top of her chest, to her collarbone. For many months she had used every ounce of her mental energy to help Rea figure out her ability, modeling physics equations and trying to solve them. When that wasn't enough, she'd broken into a US Army computer to find the data she needed to keep working toward understanding. Cora even made arrangements with the fertility clinic to ship some of the sperm she'd banked to Rea, so they could have a baby. Cora loved Rea.

She put down the weight and felt her convictions pulsing inside of her, pushing up against her fear, anger, and uncertainty. Cora set her eyes ahead, squatted down, straightened her back, and placed her hands on the bar, ready to lift again, training to do whatever she had to do when the time came.

CHAPTER 11.

Rea and Cora were torn out of sleep by heavy pounding on the door. Moments before, they had been lying close together in bed in the early-morning light.

It was so early in the morning that Cora felt barely awake. She thought it might be a delivery. She made her way downstairs, wearing a cut up t-shirt and pajama shorts, and opened the door without thinking to ask who it was.

"I am Agent Graham with the Department of Homeland Security. We have a warrant to search the premises. Step aside." The agent held a sheet of paper in one hand and rested the other on his gun. Cora squinted in her sleepy confusion, opened the door, and stepped back against the wall.

A group of agents rushed into the apartment, and Graham began to bark commands. He was wearing a bulletproof vest, over a polo shirt and khakis. He looked like he probably worked at a desk almost every day of his life, and this was the biggest thrill he'd had in a long time. The other agents wore similar uniforms, some with black cargo pants, a woman wearing a tight ponytail.

"Get in the kitchen!" Graham snapped at Cora and gestured. Cora obeyed; he followed her in. "Place your hands on the table. I have some questions for you."

Cora was awake now, pulsing in full, adrenaline-filled terror. She was aware that she was sitting in the kitchen in her pajamas in front of a federal agent. Perhaps it was dissociation or perhaps it was clarity, but she found it remarkable that she hadn't thought to put any clothes on. She had never really expected DHS to actually show up at her house, but in her fearful imaginings of this moment, she had not imagined she'd be wearing tiny sleeping shorts that were not even very cute. The morning light in the kitchen looked like it did any other day. But there was an agent with a gun standing right in front of her. In Rea's kitchen. And asking her questions. These were her thoughts when the agent's voice broke through again.

"Did you hear me? I asked, did you or did you not illegally access a US Army computer on the night of February 6th? If you answer my questions, this will go much easier for you and your girlfriend," Graham said.

As he said that, he looked to his left. Cora followed his gaze. She could see that an agent had brought Rea out of her bedroom, and was telling her to stand against the wall and put her hands above her head. The agent was a woman. She was no less mean than Graham, but Cora knew that the fact that they were still alive owed much to their privilege as people who were not Black or Indigenous.

Trans women like them were murdered or imprisoned daily. Cora considered the difference in the number of photons reflected by her and Rea's Latinx skin with those reflected by the more melanated skin of a Black person. How had their skin color been perceived by these agents and fed into their calculations of threat? How were these perceptions supported by the policing vision in their auglenses and by their own social prejudices?

"If you are not going to answer my questions, Mr. Rodriguez, we will have to take you into custody for interfering with an active investigation," said Graham.

Cora looked the agent in the eye, feeling intense fury at the dehumanizing violence of being referred to as a gender that clearly did not correlate with her body. In fact, she thought, that isn't even my legal gender any longer; this fucker must have looked far back into my records. Continuing to stare down the agent, Cora said the only words she would say to him that morning, "I have the right to remain silent."

Agents were tearing Rea's home apart. Two agents walked out the front door carrying electronic equipment, including their printer and video projector, and armfuls of paper with equations scribbled across them, as three other agents threw seat covers off the couch, tossed books off the shelves, snapped apart picture frames, and rifled through drawers. Graham stood looking off distantly and tilted his head methodically, surely directing an analysis visualization, as his fingers on his right hand twitched slightly, activating options only he could see.

Rea still stood against the wall, hands pressed firmly against it, holding her body strongly as she looked at Cora for support. Cora rested her head on the kitchen table. This was too terrible to watch, but it was also surreal. Why was she sitting in front of this agent in Rea's kitchen? She had no sense of time, and her auglenses refused to turn on. The agents must have used a proximity disabling code that the manufacturers had built into the firmware. Cora had read about how law enforcement could disable certain electronics devices, such as cell phones, within a given radius thanks to collaboration from big tech corporations. She just had not expected she would experience it. She was in her girlfriend's home, feeling naked and like she had lost part of her vision, too.

After what felt like an interminably long time—or was it just minutes? Cora couldn't tell, Graham left the kitchen without saying anything to Cora. He walked toward the door, speaking to someone over a communication link she could not see. Cora gathered that there were other agents nearby, outside the apartment, that he was coordinating with. Those inside the apartment quietly filtered out the door ahead of him, and he was the last to exit, closing the door behind him. Cora was so confused that she sat there for a moment and listened to car doors slamming shut and cars driving away. She jumped up and ran to Rea, who moved toward her too, into an embrace.

"I'm so sorry," Cora said.

"I can't believe I got you into this. *I'm* sorry!" Rea said.

"What the fuck was that?" Cora said.

"I can't believe what they did to my home!" Rea said, looking around them. They were speaking over each other now.

"My god, we're still here," Cora said. "Why didn't they arrest us?"

Rea interrupted Cora and held her tighter. "I am just so, so glad I get to hold you again." They each breathed a sigh of relief.

"They found me. I don't know how, but they found my hack," said Cora.

The agents must not yet have had enough evidence for an arrest warrant. But they both knew that it was only a matter of time.

The next day, Cora and Rea tried to go back to their lives. What had happened was so terrifying and so extreme, they didn't yet know how to integrate it. They talked about the raid a few times and talked to Cora's brother about it, too. It had been so traumatic for Rea—whose father had been in prison through much of her life—that she had disassociated intensely while the agents were in Rea's apartment, and now couldn't remember many of the details. For her part, Cora was worried that Rea would blame her, so she didn't bring the incident up often. She was afraid to rock the boat. Cora knew that she had probably gone too far in her attempts to prove her love to Rea, and she felt guilty about both the hack and the raid. Still, she tried to reassure Rea.

"Don't worry, babe, my encryption is solid," Cora had said once, over a dinner of homemade arepas stuffed with carne asada and avocado.

Licking the salsa off her fingers, Rea said, "I know, hun. I know you're brilliant. But this is Homeland Security we're talking about here, and this new right-wing administration does not care about your rights or mine."

"Totally! I know! That's why I encrypted everything with a decryption key that can only be accessed by my auglenses, with my biosignature. I encrypted the partition. I encrypted the files, and after the hack, I deleted all the evidence of it, the code, the malware executable, the shell commands. There is no trace left."

Rea paused between bites, holding the hot cornmeal patty in her hand. "I trust you, Cora," she said, finally. "We'll be ok. I'm still going to talk to my friends in the Lawyer's Guild to see if they can help us, in case—"

"Sure, yes! Please talk to them. But I don't think they are ever coming back. There's no way they can gather any evidence from what they took." She sat back in her chair, then laughed and said, "Especially not from the video projector."

Over the next month, they struggled to get back to normalcy, even though Rea had a new irritability about her. The raid had heightened her fears of losing Cora. Rea told Cora that she had been struggling to feel grounded.

One thing they did want to talk about, still, was having a child. It had been a dream of Cora's for so long, and for Rea it had been a dream that circumstances had already interrupted several times. Now they worked together less on the solution to their quantum probability problem, having lost a lot of their progress in the raid, and spent more time cuddling, sharing their visions of their future together, and walking Azul. When they discussed what they might name her—or alternately mused on having a boy instead of a girl—they both smiled warmly and laughed. It seemed like a dream to them, even when they were discussing their fears. They talked about parenting methods and wrote up budgets for the duration of pregnancy and their child's first year. It was all happening too soon, but it felt so necessary.

Cora had read many times that the average life expectancy for a trans woman is thirty-five years old. The computer scientist in her was skeptical of that number, knowing that data collection on transgender health was still poor. Due to discrimination and transphobia, most doctor's offices still only asked patients if they were male or female. So as far as Cora was concerned, any speculation about the short life expectancy of transgender women was skewed by the fact that many trans women lived invisible lives. They only become worthy of counting and recordkeeping when murdered, and even then, they were still often misgendered.

Still, despite her own logic, that number reached a very deep kind of fear far inside of her. Cora was just about to turn thirty-five and felt that any days that she kept living were days that she was lucky to have. Her age—and the thought of how little time she might have left—made her desire to have a child with Rea feel even more urgent. She knew they hadn't known each other long enough to be making these plans, but taking more time to build trust felt like a luxury that Cora couldn't afford.

On Rea's side of the baby discussions, it seemed that her yearning and openness were also driven by fear. Rea shared that it felt to her like an inescapable reality that she might slip into a different probable universe any time the two shared a particularly tender kiss, or any time they made love, as their loving connection reached profound, sacred depths. Yet on top of that, she knew Rea felt the anxiety of trauma, like a static field buzzing at her, from her worry that Cora would be arrested. She wanted to trust in Cora's technical genius, she said, and that she wanted to believe in the power of Cora's direct action to protect her rights with *encryption* instead of "the law." But Rea never let go of the fear the government had access to technologies and forensic methods beyond what Cora knew.

Cora was aware major tech companies created backdoors to their own security software for law enforcement's use, so she relied on open-source encryption software. And she relied also on the mathematicians and other intellectuals who, as proof of their belief in privacy rights, studied encryption software for flaws. But in this new and violent situation, everyone had become targets and principles seemed to recede daily in the face of multiplying threats.

How many family members needed to be threatened to make someone stop acting on their values? How precarious did someone's family have to be before those principles felt much more flexible? How many people under this new regime were employed imprisoning children in cages at the border in order to feed their own children? With stakes like these, the right to privacy faded away quickly. Security has always been guaranteed to the rich, and it was becoming far, far more costly every day.

CHAPTER 12.

A soulful electronic bassline woke me up from sleep—my phone's alarm with its text, "Good morning, Rea," flashing. I opened my eyes, feeling Cora's warm body next to mine, still unmoving. The bassline created a grounding, like swaying over firmly planted legs, while a higher pitch with a brighter timbre traveled in a slow arc above it. The French sound of the band Air had been my wakeup tone for a while now, allowing for a gentle awakening. But the brightness of the light coming in through the blinds confused me. I had lately begun to keep my phone in the next room, both for better sleep and to make me get out of bed to turn off the alarm.

Groggily walking into the living room, I picked up my phone and saw that I had set the alarm incorrectly the night before, and had overslept by an hour. It was rare that I overslept, since Cora usually jumped out of bed early to head to the gym. When I dismissed the alarm, I saw the text message on my screen.

"SHIT WHERE ARE YOU THE FEDS ARE HERE LOOKING FOR YOU," the capitals screamed. It was a message from my friend Estrella, whom I worked with at school.

My stomach dropped out of this world, my eyes opened wide, and my mind flew away from my body out the top of my head. I stepped backward, staring at the text for a long moment, and then pulled myself back together, my feelings packed down into a tight ball in my stomach. I knew what

I had to do. I put the phone down and walked back to the bedroom.

As I entered the room, Cora opened her eyes, looked at me, and stretched her whole body, quietly groaning with pleasure. I crawled onto the bed, holding myself up on my hands and knees, and kissed Cora.

"Oh, good morning!" Cora said, pulling away after a long, deep kiss, and smiled. "I thought you had to rush off to work."

"I'm not going anywhere," I replied, straddling Cora's legs. We began to kiss again. I knew those words were my deepest hope but were, in fact, now very low probability. I didn't have time to weigh my terror over Cora living in the violence of prison against my fear of losing her to another universe. It was too late and running seemed futile.

Still, an image of us both at the airport, fleeing from the feds, flashed into my mind. But the current state of the airport included soldiers with automatic weapons, DX-ray scanners, networks of sensors embedded throughout the terminals, and the scrutinizing auglenses of all the agents and airline staff. The scene that came to me was of the two of us at the security checkpoint holding hands, while an uncountable number of lines intersected our bodies, rays emanating from the eyes of agents, cameras, and monitoring sensors. Even the flight attendants going through the expedited security line next to us had auglenses, all trapping us both in a web of surveillance that would prevent us from escaping the country. I pushed it out of my mind by coming back into the moment. I took off my shirt and so did Cora, and we began to make love.

Our mouths moved across each other's bodies. Our fingers pressed into each other's deepest pleasures. I let all of my passion loose, set my fears aside, didn't hold back from opening completely. We both leaned into the exquisite sensation deep in our bodies, resonating through my core, as we took in each other's sweating expressions of excess. I kissed Cora again and again, came to orgasm, and then began to cry quietly. We continued to hold each other and share our bodies until Cora, too, called out in bliss. Then we fell away from each other onto the bed, sweat everywhere, panting.

I whispered to Cora, "I love you, Cora. So much."

Cora's eyes were closed as she began to drift into unconsciousness. She opened them, looked into my eyes, and said, "I love you too, Rea." Her hand brushing my cheek.

I looked at her and felt the room slowly starting to rotate. More tears streamed from my eyes in a river down the side of my face, leaving a dark spot on the sheets. Our atoms had touched, which could never happen in this universe. I reached my hand out, tried to blink away the tears, and Cora was gone.

I woke up and rolled over to look out the window of my apartment. I knew everything was changed. Through the flat gray clouds, the sun was just starting to shine through, bright rays moving along the water, refracting into gold ripples. Wide beams next to thin beams next to patches of shadow.

I checked my watch to read an email notification. Seeing the subject line, "Your package "banked tissue" has shipped from 'anonymous donor,'" sent a bolt of profound joy and profound loss through me simultaneously, knowing that this was Cora's tissue and that the email should have listed her name. I was racked with the intensity of these two powerful currents at odds inside me, like a storm. I felt my stomach muscles convulse as I cried, balling myself up, squeezing all the muscles in my face. I wailed.

After a while, I got out of bed, poured water in the kettle, turned on the gas stove. Following this ritual was the only way I was able to move. I picked up my phone and called my ex, Calley. We had dated very briefly, years ago, before my problem with the laws of physics had gotten so bad.

"Hi, Calley, how's it going?" I said.

"Good! Just submitted my app to another grad program yesterday," said Calley.

"I'm so happy for you, Calley," I said. I paused then, "Does that mean that what we talked about isn't going to work for you anymore?"

"No, girl! Don't be silly! You and I talked about having a child together so many years ago. Why?" Calley asked.

I sighed with intense relief. I didn't know if Calley still wanted to coparent, didn't know what had changed in this new universe and what had held. I was glad to learn this part of the timeline was intact. "Okay," I said, "well, I got the email today from the fertility center. This means we're going to have to be ready for the insemination soon."

"Oh my god," I heard Calley breathe. "I can't believe we are finally doing this. Okay. I'll call my OBGYN and let her know. I'm so nervous and excited!"

"I can't either, Calley, I can't either," I echoed, with a combination of absence and astonishment. "And I'll call my doctor again about the domperidone, too, so I can breastfeed."

We hung up the phone, having made plans to meet up later. The kettle was already screaming that the water was ready. I made my way into the kitchen, glanced down at the checkered tiles, and immediately they began to warp. Scared and confused, I jerked my eyes away from the dizzying pattern and scrambled to turn off the stove. Out the kitchen window, I saw snow.

Snow in LA? But instead, I saw the backyard of my first apartment in Montreal, snow covering the plants and piling up against the fence. Behind me, I heard a baby cry. I whirled around in utter surprise and saw my kitchen in LA, just as I had seen it a moment before.

I'm losing my fucking mind, I thought. Then I heard it again, a baby—but more than that, I *felt* the baby's cry as it reached into my depths, forcing my body to react. I stepped into my living room, and there, below the recently replaced diagrams of waveforms and equations, was a crib. I backed into my kitchen and looked out the window again. Still LA. Then the baby cried a third time, and I went to the crib.

In the crib, I saw a beautiful, swaddled and crying new-born. The baby's face was red and wrinkled with only the tini-est of dark hairs on its head. I picked the baby up and cradled it in my arms. I began to bounce the baby ever so slightly and sing to it. Pacing the room, I rocked the baby, singing and humming a song I made up on the spot. After a while, the baby stopped crying, and I sat on the couch. My phone rested in the folds of a gray throw on the couch, and I looked at the glowing reminder that came through: "Calley picking up baby—Tomorrow, 8 a.m."

I wrinkled my brow, drawn out of my reverie into the frustration of total confusion, trying to understand. The baby in my lap fussed and cried again; I checked its diaper. Trying to soothe the baby, I said, "I'll call you Jorge, after Borges . . . or maybe Luis, in case you decide to change it to Luisa. Both are beautiful names, and he's one who certainly fits this moment." I held the infant and looked out the window toward the bay. Before my eyes, the light shifted from late morning to sunrise, the colors going from bright daylight sunshine to an early orange glow, like an accelerated sunset in reverse. I felt a deep fear in my chest. I had shifted between universes before but never experienced this kind of rapid slipping between so many possibilities.

I felt a warmth on my nipple—I looked down and saw the baby was weeks older now, in my arms and breastfeed-ing. I sunk back down onto the couch, bewildered, and looked at my phone again. The alert had changed: "Calley picks up Luis—Saturday, 10 a.m." I was tumbling through realities fast.

CHAPTER 13.

Cora said a nervous thank you to the flight crew as she stepped off the plane in Bogotá. Walking through the airport, she remarked that it was similar to the one she had left. Due to the increased militarization of US borders and airports, the presence of soldiers with machine guns in these places seemed normal to Cora, although still alarming. And they were especially alarming because she had just deleted millions of criminal records on the plane from law enforcement databases all across the US in her hack of the LEAP portal, and she was still carrying the hardware she'd used for the hack. She collected her suitcases from baggage claim, and wheeled them to customs. Thanks to Colombia's status as one of the top recipients of military aid from the US government, here customs had a DX-ray scanner.

She had only been to Bogotá once, for work and then only virtually. From that meeting, though, she had learned of the city's growing media art scene, with many artists innovating in VR and AR. After the peace accords between the government and the Revolutionary Armed Forces of Colombia, the country was beginning the long slow road to repair. Cora thought she'd be safer after the hack if she was geographically far from the US, and she knew she wanted to be in Latin America.

When she saw Carmen Lopera elected, Bogotá's first openly lesbian mayor, she thought that might be the city to move to. It seemed that perhaps Colombia was one of the most progressive places in Latin America. When she started looking for places to live, and saw images of Bogotá, it seemed dreamy, and she decided to land there.

The war on drugs had generated incredible profits for weapons and aircraft manufacturers, as well as for the information technology companies that supplied Colombia's army and police with powerful new digital tools. In Bogotá, her luggage was moving through the same kind of digital device scanner they had used in the US. Armed police stood closely by, as soldiers with German Shepherds walked past while the dogs sniffed Cora for illegal drugs. The intensity of her fear felt like a screaming winter wind in her mind, which made it seem like the sweat on her lower back was freezing, despite the warmth of the humid air.

Cora mentally reviewed all the precautions she had taken: she had used a random-access memory (RAM) drive for her log directory, to make certain that her command history was not stored—data in RAM exists only temporarily and is never written to a hard drive. She had used strong encryption, too, so the contents of the RAM drive wouldn't be easy to pry into. And she had used a temporary operating system on a USB 4.0 drive to boot her laptop and auglens connections. Then, she made sure to power down completely and reboot, so that the RAM was refreshed with a new and harmless array of contents—standard news websites and boring work email.

One of the guards pulled Cora's bag off the belt. "Señora, ven aquí por favor," he instructed.

The guard walked Cora over to the explosive chemical detector, which was connected to an advanced DX-ray with the power to comb through the contents of her device in greater detail. After a long silence, as the guard pawed through the contents of her bag while a soldier on duty paced occasionally behind her with an automatic rifle in hand, he spoke to her again.

"Tiene salchicha aquí?" he asked.

Cora was so flustered that the word didn't translate in her mind. She sweated and stammered, "Ahh . . . I . . . "

The guard looked at her disdainfully, seeing her now as a girl from the US who didn't even know her own people's language. In sarcastic English he asked, "You got sausage in here?"

She felt her stomach twist, but her brow furrowed as fear quickly converted to anger. "I have a dildo in there," she said.

The guard stopped, a pair of her panties still in his hand, and peered again at the X-ray image in his auglens. He could make out the outline of the dildo—actually Cora's dilator, the medical device that trans women use to maintain their vaginal structure after surgery. He stopped and didn't look Cora in the eye again when he said, "Estas libre. You're free to go." The guard walked off, while the other soldier nearby continued to stroll past with slow wide steps, trying to maintain the theater of security. Cora stuffed her clothes back into her bag, hastily zipping it up.

The arrivals lobby was very different here than in US airports. It was packed with families bearing signs with names on them, balloons, and celebrations as people found relief as their family members shuttled off her flight, returning home safely from a country practically at war with Latin America. The people here knew that hatred of immigrants had reached such an intense fervor in the US, with thousands of people being rounded up daily in ICE raids; just looking Colombian, much less having a Colombian accent, was enough to place their families in danger. Governments from Mexico to Chile had issued warnings to their citizens traveling abroad that the new US administration might target them, and advised returning as quickly as possible.

She watched as parents reunited with their children—her family had never supported her in this way. And she herself had always wanted children, but it had never worked out. She'd rarely even had a girlfriend or friend come to pick her up. She walked to the taxi stand and into a licensed taxi.

"Avenida calle setenta y dos, número cinco, por favor." She would never be going back so the four thousand US dollars she had saved now had to last her until she figured out how to make an income here. She hoped that the new mayor might do more for the lower income residents of the city.

"Claro, señora." Cora was relieved not to be misgendered. In fact, she even enjoyed being called "señora" with no hesitation. The road from the airport was long and flat, passing numerous short office buildings with names of businesses she didn't recognize. This was different from Mexico City, she thought, more like Miami, where the airport is outside the city. As they entered the city, Bogotá looked like a complex city in the clouds, held in the arms of mountains wearing nimbus clouds for collars.

As the amber streetlights pulsed by in rapid succession, Cora moved her head and her fingers discreetly in the dark of the back seat. The driver couldn't see her flipping through the settings interface of her auglenses. She disabled airplane mode and turned on her various wireless signal receivers, choosing Movistar, a local cellular network. A new chat notification popped up:

#sirc @nepantla: diosa_andriode, I know you're in Bogotá. I am too. I want to meet f2f. I want to help.

A message from nepantla? Wanting to meet face to face? She was surprised. The random hacker she had bought some accounts from was in Bogotá.

She looked past the floating user interface to the buildings. The auglenses registered the change in focal length in her iris, and dimmed the UI to a faint outline. They had now entered the city itself. More than seven million people lived in Bogotá, but most of the streets seemed very narrow to Cora. Outside, the streetlights cast an eerie pall on the garage doors covered in gorgeous, elaborate graffiti pieces painted on corrugated steel.

Blue-green fluorescent lights lit up a restaurant window. And there were so many people on the street. Cora was nervous and wondered if this driver was taking her to the right place. This neighborhood seemed an unlikely setting for an expensive historic hotel that regularly hosted parties for major corporations. She wanted to enjoy herself these first few days while she searched for an apartment, so she had chosen a comfortable place to stay. Now she just hoped to make it there.

Where the fuck was this hacker nepantla from, and why were they here? How was it possible that this person she'd had a single interaction with now happened to be in the same city where Cora was headed? Are they a cop? Could they have followed her from the US? As they waited at a red light, Cora anxiously retraced the security precautions she had taken when she bought the accounts from nepantla.

Rain started to fall over Bogotá, and Cora realized that the streets were filled with young people. Some still had their uniforms on and must have been high school students, hanging out together at night. She spotted a group of punk girls covering their heads from the rain with their backpacks, not wanting their purple and blue hair dye to run. A scooter sped past and stopped ahead of the line of cars waiting for the light to change.

Gradually, the buildings they passed began to look more like the financial district, taller and with colorful lights. Her taxi pulled up to the Artisan behind a line of town cars. People filled the all-glass front entrance of the tall, skinny hotel. There was clearly an event tonight. Cameras flashed at celebrities in front of a step-and-repeat patterned with logos. Cora strode briskly by them in annoyance, keeping her face turned away, and headed to the counter to check in. The last thing she needed was to be in the media.

The next night, Cora decided to meet nepantla. She'd spent much of the day viewing apartments, knowing her funds were limited and hotel time was not cheap. nepantla asked to meet her in the Santa Fe barrio. It was farther south, outside of the financial district, but not as far as La Candelaria, the area popular with tourists and the people who targeted them. The address where they were to meet was near the university, which Cora thought should be safer. Mostly, though, her curiosity was piqued.

She'd supposed nepantla wasn't a cop who'd followed her because it had been Cora who had been the first to initiate contact, and how could they have jurisdiction to follow her this far? She felt reasonably confident that this person could not have knowledge of what she had done over the airplane Wi-Fi. Still, Cora was cautious. If this was a CIA agent who had somehow followed her trail after she'd hacked the law enforcement databases, then they would have jurisdiction to follow her all this way. She only hoped that her physical training would save her if she needed it. She was prepared to run, jump, and evade almost anyone who might want to chase her, she thought.

But if nepantla wasn't a cop, Cora might actually have a friend here, a fellow hacker. Cora asked the hotel's reception to order her a reliable car service. When it arrived, she got in and instructed the driver, "Carrera siete y Calle veinticuatro." It was a spot near the address where she was to meet nepantla, but in a place where there was more foot traffic, so Cora could approach from a distance in the crowd.

Cora didn't realize that long waits in traffic were normal in certain parts of the city. When after a short drive they were stopped waiting a few cycles of the same traffic light without any movement, she was surprised when the driver asked, "Quieres caminar? Estamos muy cerca, como dos cuadras. Es allí mismo, dos cuadras más." He pointed her in a direction a few blocks ahead.

As she approached Calle 24, she found the street completely full of people. At the intersection, Cora saw that Carrera 7, one of the main, multilane streets through Bogotá, was also filled with people as far as she could see in either direction. Thousands and thousands of revelers covered in blood, in tattered clothing, some with face paint on, some with gaping wounds, some with vampire teeth, slowly ambling through the street. There were a few Jokers, Harley Quinns, Ghostbusters, and Power Rangers among them. She hadn't remembered that tonight was the Saturday before Halloween. Cora took in the massive crowd of people walking together through the street, accompanied by a cacophony of laughter, screams, and the occasional fireworks exploding.

As her eyes followed the crowd off into the horizon, her attention fell on a massive building whose face was a moving digital image. Patterns of colored lines sped across the length of the building and revealed a brown-skinned woman, dressed in bright colors of green and pink, dancing and smiling. The LEDs distorted the image just enough, so the details of her clothing were obscured; Cora was left wondering if the image was authentic, or instead a commercial appropriation or parody of indigeneity.

She knew she still had much to learn about the new Caribbean context she would be living in; race, colonialism, and slavery were configured differently here than in the US, and the ongoing neocolonialism of the drug war seemed incredibly potent and present to Cora.

Cora picked her way against the flow of the crowd, avoiding the outbursts from groups of laughing teenage zombies and drunken men in hockey masks. When she arrived at the address nepantla had given her, she found herself standing before a very old building, with tall ancient, intricate wooden doors. A sign above the door read, "Mapa Teatro."

A large group of people waited outside the doors, and Cora stood curiously with them and waited. More showed up, some dressed like young hipsters, some wearing badges for a local art festival. Many in the crowd were smoking, which she hated being near, but there was nowhere to escape without losing her place. Finally, the doors opened, and the crowd entered eagerly into a dimly lit corridor, illuminated by a single, off-center light.

Cora followed the press of the crowd into a large open space in the center of the building, while others diverged up a flight of stairs. Along the back of the hall were beautiful, arched windows that opened onto another interior space. To her right, people leaned over the railing of a balcony on the floor above, holding their drinks in their hands.

Behind her were a row of tables and computers, some with old-school CRT monitors, and numerous operators diligently manipulating the screens and keyboards she could see, as well as the interfaces and virtual keyboards that only the operators could see with their auglenses. They were preparing something, but Cora has no idea what. A woman returned to her group of friends standing near Cora's and handed out numerous small cups.

"Quieres tratar?" she asked Cora.

Her look of confusion, or perhaps her being alone, must have made it clear that Cora was new here—apparently, it was obvious. That's not good, she thought.

"Gracias, pero no," Cora said, with a slight smile.

Where was nepantla? There were hundreds of people here. Any one of them could be nepantla, and Cora was conspicuously standing in the middle of the room. She felt exposed and was about to move when the lights went out. The crowd called out in joy, then quieted. Text was projected onto the largest wall, which lit the room just enough not to be total darkness.

NEOLIBERALISMO ES UN UROBOROS

What followed was a poem about an ouroboros, the ancient symbol of a snake eating its own tail. Narrating the story of the Magdelana River, the poem described how after years of war, foreign interests rushed in to create hydroelectric dams, which activists organized against in the Ríos Vivos movement. Then two spotlights focused on two women, adorned and wrapped in beige and white fabrics, suspended in the air above the crowd, dancing and gracefully rotating on multiple axes, embodying the river. One dancer swung her legs in a beautiful arc, arms above her coming together in a matching arc, while the other kicked her legs but held them straight, one arm above and the other curving out as if gesturing to the crowd. As they changed positions and began to dance upside down, Cora watched the spotlight cross over the fine cords that each one danced from. Their movements held a powerful beauty and so much bravery.

As she watched the dancers, images of the Colombian countryside faded into her vision, seemingly between her and the dancers. But when she turned her head, she saw a closer view of the river and slow images of indigenous activists narrating how the river has personhood and should be protected as fiercely as any other living being. These images were in front of Cora but not in the room; they didn't correspond to the geometry of the space she was in, but to another plane. Cora had to turn her head to try to relate to these new visuals. Then, she understood what the operators had been working on behind the tables—she was experiencing a kind of art she had never before seen.

Black-and-white representations of the city's architecture replaced the poem on the wall, using an old projection technique, real film, actual physical captures of light in silver emulsion. That alone would have been mesmerizing, but the scenes of Bogotá were overlaid with images appearing in her auglenses of the jungle along the riverside. The choreography of the women dancing—moving with strength and grace despite their precariousness hovering above the crowd—conveyed complex depictions of environmental struggle, police violence, military and paramilitary agents, and protesters trying to stop the dams. She was in awe at the expressive power of the performance.

A third dancer appeared, draped in long green and teal silks, between the crowd and the dancers above. She seemed to be on her own plane, and Cora couldn't see the wires she was suspended from. Turning her head to adjust to this new presence, added to the existing mix of moving augmented images, live performers, and projections in the room, Cora lost her bearings and began to feel dizzy. Immediately, her stomach sank. This dizziness had suddenly become a regular occurrence in the last few weeks, and sometimes she found it difficult to stand upright when the vertigo hit her. She closed her eyes and looked toward the floor; her auglenses detected the muscle contractions, and went into sleep mode behind her eyelids, allowing her the temporary relief of darkness. Still, she felt the room spinning, and she had nothing to grab onto in this crowd of people. Her breathing became short and rapid. She pressed her hand against the shoulder of a person next to her for just a moment, and they turned around.

"Perdón, con permiso . . . " she mumbled apologetically, disoriented. Cora opened her eyes again and began to navigate her way to the edge of the crowd. In the dim light of the hall, lots of people were talking, asking what others had seen in their auglenses or describing the augmented performance—auglenses were even more of a rarity not many people could afford here in Bogotá. Everything blurred together as she tried to find her balance again and feel the floor. As she reached the wall, keeping her eyes averted away from the augmented images and the dancers overhead, her vision began to stabilize. The spinning room began to slow then settle. Cora took two deep breaths to try to calm her panic. The moment was receding.

Recovering her normal breathing, Cora looked up to the second floor and saw a woman in a hood, leaning on the ornate railing, looking directly at her. The lights off the dancers reflected onto her face, letting Cora make out that her lips moved and the long curly hair pouring out of her hood. Cora had drawn attention to herself by moving through the crowd suddenly, but it was only momentary; everyone's attention quickly returned to the dancers above and the projections all around them. But this woman with dark hair like the living branches of a tree was still staring at Cora. She must be nepantla, thought Cora, then the woman turned and was gone.

Cora stayed where she was in the crowd, near the wall. A moment later, the woman stepped into the room through the entrance nearest Cora, weaved through the audience, then walked right up to her. She put her face close enough to Cora's to speak over the music of the performance, and in the shifting, bluish light Cora could see then that she was only a kid, probably fifteen or sixteen years old. That disarmed her, but also added to her confusion.

"Diosa andriode?" was all she said, loudly over the music.

Cora hesitated, looked at her one last time, considered her safety and her risk, and said, "Yes."

"Come on," said nepantla, and Cora followed her out of the hall. They navigated the narrow corridor full of increasingly drunk and raucous people. Soon, nepantla led her into a separate room at the back of the venue, which felt as expansive as the one they'd left. It had a similar layout, with an open second story, high ceilings, and a walkway around the upper floor. Palm trees spread their arms in every corner of this room, their linear fronds splayed out like bones, and echoed the tall doors built in pairs along the walls, with louvered slats making up their top halves. Here most people were drinking out of paper cups, smoking, and laughing. The light in this room was all rays and stripes. nepantla moved to a corner away from the bar where there were few people.

"Nepantla?" said Cora, when they got there.

She smiled, "Yeah, that's me. It means 'shapeshifter'— that's just one of my handles. I'm so happy to finally meet you.

Listen, it's too dangerous to talk here. I know you're running, and while this club is pretty cool, there are way too many people here to be safe. I need you to meet me tomorrow at the foot of the Bolívar monument on Carrera Revolución."

"What? Why should I trust you?" Cora said.

"I think we have someone dear to us in common," said nepantla. Something in her eyes made Cora feel like she was being honest, but she wasn't sure whom nepantla was referring to.

CHAPTER 14.

The next afternoon, Cora was standing at the foot of the huge cement column below the massive statue of Simón Bolívar on a horse. She looked up, and shielded her eyes from the sun to read the placard describing Bolívar's resistance against the Spanish colonizers in the early nineteenth century. The smell of exhaust was thick as cars sped by. Highly alert, Cora kept watch, keeping her eyes on the small sliver of green and sidewalk connecting the monument to the street. She saw the tienditas selling a mix of sugar-filled cheap candy and produce, including plantains and yucca.

As she scanned the horizon, nepantla emerged from around the corner of the monument. Cora was confused; it was impossible that she had not seen nepantla cross the street toward her. On her way to their meeting point, Cora had crossed the highway and circled the monument to check for clean-cut gringos or anyone with excessively clean shoes—traits that she thought might give an undercover agent away.

nepantla walked up to Cora, her big hood pulled over her head, hair spilling out around her face. She came close enough to speak over the sound of the highway and said, "Call me Os. That's my actual name. And come this way."

Cora followed her around to the back side of the monument, the side with traffic rushing away from it. Then, to Cora's surprise, Os pushed a door open that had seemed to be just crack in the old, soot-covered wall. The door led to a staircase, and Cora closed the door behind her as they descended. They arrived at a platform lit with faint glows of green and purple. On the platform stood a scruffy, muscular punk of indeterminate gender in an old black denim jacket, covered in patches, smoking a cigarette, and mentally buried in their phone, which they held sideways and close to their face, typing furiously with both thumbs. Os and Cora passed them, and went down a second set of stairs.

As they descended, they entered a large space lit by a handful of fluorescent tube lights that were scattered across tables covered in sheets of brown paper and electronics parts. As they reached the bottom of the staircase, Cora noticed that on the wall to the right of them, a wave of purple and green dots of light was fluctuating, depicting two human forms in the center. In the middle of the room facing the mirage of colors, Cora saw someone hunched over a laptop screen, a 3-D scanner on the adjacent table. And someone else was standing behind them, gesturing to the mirage and saying something about waveforms.

On the left side of the room, a woman in jeans, leather boots, and a long, dark blue technical rain jacket leaned against a wall and put her face up against what looked like a crack that pale blue light was shining out of, as if she was peering through a peephole. Three others stood together at the back of the room, discussing something loudly over a mess of papers, stickies, and images from books and magazines laying across a table.

"What is that?!" Cora asked in slow astonishment at the shimmering purple and green field that seemed to hover above the wall on their right.

"It's a projection mapping art installation—" Os answered reflexively, then caught herself, remembering who she was talking to. "No. Really, it's sort of a portal that we're working on. Let me explain . . . "

Os gestured for Cora to follow her to the tables illuminated by fluorescent tubes. Cora saw they were covered in large sheets of butcher paper, and she felt she recognized the hand-written physics equations on them, but she couldn't exactly place where from. Why were they so familiar?

"Are you aware of the many worlds interpretation of quantum physics?" asked Os. She pointed to a large sheet paper on which was scrawled, in red grease pencil:

$$\mu i \equiv \langle \Psi_{UNIVERSE} \mid Pi \mid \Psi_{UNIVERSE} \rangle$$

"What geek isn't?" said Cora with a bit of geek bravado, hiding her astonishment and her uneasiness at the sense her memory was failing her. "You can read about it almost any week on *io*9," she said. It wasn't exactly l33t, but the flex helped her feel less uncertain.

Os pulled back her hood, revealing the intricate pattern she had created around her eyes with black and green eyeliner and silver eye shadow. Her gaze was affectionate.

"I've always wanted to understand the deepest secrets of the world. I've always been fascinated by the laws that shape reality and finding out how to bend them. I must have gotten it from my bio parents because I certainly didn't get it from any of my other caretakers," Os explained. "As far back as I can remember, I was devouring books of mythology, religion, poetry, and later philosophy and science. I see the goddess in these sweeping, graceful equations as much as I see her in the braided branches of trees with black crows squawking in them," Os said and ran her hand across the equation before her. Then she turned and looked at Cora, searching.

"I didn't know why, but I remember from my youngest days that my mom was desperate to solve these equations. I remember her telling me about the woman she loved, who was far away and totally inaccessible to her," Os paused here. "I couldn't understand when I was little, but when I was taken away from her, studying these equations was my way of trying to get back to my mom, trying to be close to her. So, I worked on learning the math and the coding skills I needed to be able to understand them, and in the process, I found something," said Os. To Cora, it seemed like Os had been preparing for this moment for a long time. Os's expression was filled with so much hope as she spoke.

Os picked up one of the fluorescent tube lights and moved it across the table. She shone it on another equation at the center of the table, which had been circled wildly in red grease pencil and had many lines in other colors extending out from it toward other equations. Os waited for Cora to read it. Cora's furrowed her brow and drew closer to the paper. She started moving her left hand in the air quickly in an angular motion, flicked her fingers, then finally drew a graceful wave, calling up a model to verify the equation in her auglenses. When she finished, Cora looked straight at Os. Os said nothing, waiting for Cora to initiate.

Cora did not speak but traced her hand to the equations above the one in the center, verifying Os's logic. Periodically she interacted with an aug model, checking. She returned to the central equation frantically, mumbling to herself. "The differential . . . the observer . . . universe i . . . reality $alpha$ . . . " Then her expression changed to one of clear, open understanding.

After a long pause surveying the array of equations, Cora looked back at Os. "This is some impressive thinking, kid, but you're starting with an impossible assumption."

Os flinched slightly at the diminutive way Cora had referred to her, and her smile dropped. "And what do you find impossible?"

"Your observer, the variable you've named m, has access to two different realities, two different complete universes. By passing from the first to the next, your observer breaks the completeness of each universe," Cora said.

"And why should we assume that an observer can't cross from one reality to the next? Who is to say that the completeness of each universe disallows the addition of an observer who exists in both as a result of having crossed from one to another?" said Os, with too much confidence. "I think *your* assumption that an observer can't cross is the limitation in your thinking that is making this clearly evidenced solution seem impossible to you! What's impossible is your comprehension, not the possibility," Os replied, quickly getting frustrated.

Without a word, Cora turned her attention back to the table and resumed poring over the equations, moving her left hand in a slow arc with tiny movements of her fingers.

After a moment, Os asked, "Have you ever donated sperm to a tissue bank?"

Cora stepped back from the table, her face darkening as she receded from the light. "What is wrong with you? That is personal. I'm not asking you about your medical history. Fuck this. I am out of here!"

She turned to leave when Os shouted after her urgently, "Do you remember Rea?"

The name stopped Cora in her tracks. By now, all the other hackers had stopped to watch the drama unfolding between her and Os. Cora thought that they must have seen others before her brought down here and introduced to the idea of an expansive multiverse. But this sudden divergence in the line of questioning toward her personal history seemed to confuse everyone else as well. A woman working at the laptop controlling the portal chided Os, "Que es eso, chica? ¿Porque están molestando ella?"

Cora heard the comment as if through a vast silence. The name "Rea" had opened a crater in her chest, and Cora felt so much grief and so much longing.

"Realidad," said Os, and the word echoed through that dark, cavernous room studded with screens dancing with code and images of waveforms.

It was subtle, the nearly imperceptible feeling of her neurons reconnecting after having been severed by a quantum interaction that caused her displacement into a different reality.

Like the mirage image shimmering on the wall, Cora felt a memory shifting into place.

She thought of a protest she had been at in LA, one against the fascist being elected president. She didn't know why that memory was suddenly replaying in her mind, but she remembered a new detail she had never noticed before. A new neural pattern allowed her to recall more of that memory than she ever had before. She remembered standing close to the riot cops as they beat back protesters. She remembered the shattered light of sirens, headlights, and helicopters that created a vortex of color and the horizon seeming to toss back and forth. She remembered backing away from the cops as she recorded them in her auglenses, and a woman approaching her, showing her concern.

She remembered that woman's face now as if she was gazing into it with love, and she knew that it was Realidad she was remembering meeting for the first time. Cora steadied herself and looked back at Os.

"How?" she asked.

"I think I'm *observer m*," said Os. "I'm the one who crossed over."

CHAPTER 15.

I had been holding Luis, the baby, in my arms, watching the walls slowly change shape and color, from navy blue to pink to forest green back to off-white to slate gray, for what seemed like weeks, or was it years? The house I was in finally stopped shifting. I sat on the couch.

I was experiencing so many moments in this place between universes. I lay on the carpet with Luis playing with him, with his bright colored mat and toys, trying to teach him to hold himself up. Again and again, playing, making sounds with the bright red maraca, teaching Luis to turn his head, to hold the maraca, to shake it himself. I played my favorite music for him, introducing to him the songs I loved, from Fleetwood Mac to Beyoncé to Depeche Mode, even finding baby versions played on xylophones. I was a mother now. I wanted to show Luis the most beautiful parts of life. I held him in my arms and danced with him to "Tiny Dancer," which he looked confused about at first, but he began to enjoy it, smiling and laughing.

He cried; he screamed. Luis cried for hours, days, months. Did he just have gas, or was he also feeling the world impossibly spinning and shifting around us? I held him and tried my best to soothe him. I swung him gently back and forth in my arms, as the light outside our windows shifted from a bright morning to a deep, otherworldly orange.

"Shh, sh, sh, sh, sh, sh, sh, shhhhh . . . " I tried to soothe him with the sounds I had learned should calm him.

Gazing outside as I held him, I felt him start to relax. I smelled smoke and saw that on the mountains in the distance wildfires burned, not very far from our home. As time dilated and contracted around us, I witnessed climate change happening right outside my window, and it filled me with intense dread. The orange light gave way to black skies, the fires faded, and I calmed down and felt Luis calm down with me. I knew that I had to hold this baby through whatever was happening in the world. Then the world lurched again. The sun passed impossibly fast, a dim ball batted across the sky, the sky returned to normal blues then slipped into a deep indigo, slowing once again.

There were thousands of diaper changes. Again and again, in the morning, in the middle of the night. And there were hard moments, the hardest. I woke up to Luis crying in the middle of the night, again. So tired—it had been how long? I had no idea how many hundreds of times I had woken up to his crying. I didn't really sleep anymore, so often worried if he was still breathing and if I was doing this right. Sleep felt mostly like getting a nap for a few hours before he needed another bottle or a diaper change. This time, I was far past the end of my endurance.

Why won't you stop crying? Why won't you sleep? Luis had woken up every forty minutes, it seemed. As I looked down at him on the changing table, I felt so many feelings: anger, shame over feeling angry, frustration, judgment of myself for not being more patient. I talked through it, "I'm taking off your diaper. I'm getting you clean now. Hold on, baby, just another moment. Stay there. I'm picking up your butt and putting the diaper underneath you. I'm putting on your new diaper." This helped us both, helped me ground through the swirl of emotion and helped him calm down, hearing my voice. I finished, picked him up, and started rocking him in my arms. Again, like so many times before, I sang to him quietly.

"I just called to say I love you. I just called to say how much I care," I sang, learning to soothe myself at the same time. I felt that even if the world was ending outside, this was the most meaningful thing for me to be doing right now.

Then I was feeding him again, tenderly holding the bottle for him, his eyes closed—so peaceful—his tiny hands reaching out for me. I had fed him countless times already. The light was the dim light of twilight, everything blue, just after sunset. In the darkening room, Luis fed and slowly fell asleep. Finally, I thought, he was calm, the fires and the smoke storm had passed. In that moment, I felt so much love for him. In that short respite from the churning reality outside, I noticed how ordinary it was, sitting on my couch, holding Luis after he had drifted off. This was the best moment of my life. I wanted it to last forever.

Days later, lying on the ground again with Luis, I thought that this couldn't last, that it was slipping away. I watched Luis start to push himself up, then bounce himself up from the knees, balancing on his hands, and eventually learning to crawl. He crawled slowly, tentatively toward his stuffed bunny. I played *Clair de Lune* by Debussy for him. As Luis crawled toward my face, laughing his tiny, adorable laugh, I became overwhelmed with the beauty of life. I was simultaneously attuned to my boundless love for him, and the knowledge that we couldn't stay together, in this place that was shifting between so many universes. It was cinematic.

It had become impossible to perceive the passage of time. At times, days passed in seconds. Luis crawled out of the room and walked back in. I started to cry. I was sure I was losing my mind now, but I wanted to hold on, to stay here. A cover of the Pixies for babies played on the speaker, chimed notes filling in for lyrics—where is my mind? The gleaming rose clouds outside of a continuously morphing sunset could've been a hurricane or a vast otherworldly sky folding in on itself. All spirals and folds, sustaining the same time of day for an unnaturally long time. I had read that climate change would create worsening storms and now I watched as an impossibly large vortex filled the sky. Luis came into the room, older now, perhaps eight years old—I was having a hard time placing it. His face even seemed to shimmer as he spoke to me. Was he twelve now?

"Mama, quiero decirte algo . . . " he said with a soft voice, and I felt that he wanted to let me know he had something to say that he was deeply shy about sharing.

"Of course, babe, please tell me. You can tell me anything," I said through my tears, trying to hold on to the moment for him. I noticed he wore only a long t-shirt. Was he wearing pajamas? Was it morning? My eyes darted back to the unreal sky.

"I don't want to wear pants anymore. Please don't make me. Por favor, mami, I want you to call me 'she' and I want my name to be Luz," and she, Luz, started to cry then as well. She mirrored my sadness and fear with her own.

I was shocked that Luz felt she had to hide this or had to cry about it. I felt a sudden dawning joy. Joy that Luz was finding herself. Joy that Luz had wanted to share this new part of herself with me, and joy that I had held on long enough to experience this painfully beautiful moment of bravery and life with her. I held Luz's face tenderly in my hands, kissed her forehead, and pulled her in to hug her.

"Of course, mija, Luz. You can be who you want to be. I love you. I will always love you, no matter where we are, even if we are separated across universes. I love you, Luz."

Luz looked up at me, our eyes meeting, a small, tender smile dawning from beneath her tears. Luz hugged me and held me so tightly. In the time that followed, time that seemed like days extending into weeks, Luz asked me to buy her dresses. They showed up in packages at our door in unpredictable intervals: frilly purple dresses, cute patterned dresses to match my own, and lots of barrettes and tiaras. I taught my daughter to brush her hair and to braid it. I supported Luz in ways that I never was.

One night, as I was getting Luz ready for bed, brushing her hair in the mirror, I looked out the window and saw bright daylight running across the trees, patterned by the clouds—unnaturally fast. I could feel that the world was slipping again. From the window, I looked back at Luz, and she faded out of existence. Everything went quiet. The world was still. It was night again.

"No. No—" I stammered. I felt the teardrops well, filling my vision, and then fall. Reality had returned, but when I lost Luz, I felt the world break. I examined the wall of my home. It was a solid off-white, not warped or slanted; it was single story, and it was not moving. Outside of the window, it was a cold, cloudless night with a few stars shining in the sky. Their light twirled, flickered slightly, as stars do. Somewhere, something had happened to stop my falling through the endless possible universes, but I didn't know what it was, or who had caused it. I only knew that my world had ended.

CHAPTER 16.

Shattered. I was shattered by having lost Luz. Even though I knew it couldn't last, when the end came, it was no less painful. The only relief was in knowing that the worst thing in the world had happened to me, and that nothing worse could happen now. I cried so hard I couldn't breathe, cried until my head was splitting, lay on the couch staring at nothing until I cried some more. I thought I had known what suffering was, but I was wrong. Nothing hurt like this did.

Yet I went on, and now that time passed normally again, I was able to reach out to my friends. I knew they couldn't truly understand what had happened to me, so I told them that I had lost someone dear to my heart. Xandra came over the next day and helped me pick up my house. The kid's toys had disappeared as if my child had never existed, but the place was still a mess. It was hard to move at all, and Xandra moved things with me. We talked. I tried to explain what I could without outing myself or sounding insane. Xandra did what was most important, what I most needed: she just sat with me, held my hand, and cried with me. She got me through those first days. My dear Maca drove me where I needed to go, and even though she couldn't relate to my story, it helped. Maca took me on walks with her kids—being with them was painful, but still it helped.

I thought of Luz every day, hundreds of times a day. I woke up thinking about her and where she was and what happened to her, and I went to bed thinking about her. I tried to draw some pictures of her, but I'd never been very good at drawing. Some nights, I would dream about playing with her, holding her, then wake up to the devastating reality that she was gone.

All I could do was breathe. It was a monumental effort to make food or to clean or do anything to care for myself. But I could breathe. And gradually I started meditating. I read books by Buddhists like Thich Nhat Hanh, whose words were so gentle. I needed all of that kindness just to carry myself through the days. I sat and breathed and felt my chest rising, my stomach expanding then falling and contracting, again and again. And I cried and tried to hold myself with tenderness. Yes, I felt stupid and hated the universe at times, but I tried, when I could, to come back to breathing.

My sweet dog Azul was always there for me. She would sit next to me on the couch, watching me with her sweet, brown, soulful eyes. Some nights, I just lay on the floor, crying, hugging Azul in a full body embrace. I think she knew that I was hurting. And I know she loved the attention, even if I still didn't let her lick my face.

From breathing, I moved on to walking. Again, my friends carried me through. I finally learned to have meaningful, vulnerable, connected friendships. Walking and looking at the ocean with Hana, walking and looking at the trees with Maca, walking and listening to the birds with Xandra. Maca and I walked Azul down the long winding path by the park near our apartments. I loved to stop to listen to the symphony of birdsong and peer up at the tall trees that looked to be embracing each other tenderly.

Over the next year, I slowly found life and beauty again. There was a huge oak tree in my neighborhood, and I made regular journeys to visit it. I slowly began to see life in the world and see the spirit of the universe in the ocean, the moon, the stars. I realized that by causing an intentional shift between universes to save Cora, I had almost broken the laws of physics—or at least my place in them. My best guess was that it was that shift that had precipitated my falling through many, many universes. And in those other timelines, I had witnessed many possibilities of climate collapse.

The news and scientific reports had long made it clear that we were on a precipice, that global climate change would worsen if we continued on with capitalism as we know it; we also knew it could be restored if we, urgently, reduced emissions. It seemed like a matter of probability, a huge system with so many variables. But slipping through possible realities, seeing the wildfires come so close to my home while I held Luz in my arms, I knew that I had to focus, had to do everything I could to stop it. For her.

I decided to devote myself to an expansive vision of climate justice. And I resolved to try to stop whatever I was doing to create these shifts between universes, to prevent any damage I might be causing. I began to focus my research at the university on ecofeminist critiques, examining the ways that racism, sexism, and colonialism were the underpinnings of our climate catastrophe. In my free time, I joined friends doing activism for climate justice. A local anarchist collective focused on social ecology was putting on a street theater production—a parade of wildlife threatened by prison construction—and I pitched in. Constructing duck costumes and swan puppets brought me the first joy I had felt in a long time.

For years after, I stayed single, which seemed like the safest course of action. I finally realized that it was not worth losing the world, losing my reality, for romance. Maybe I just didn't meet anyone who felt worth the risk, now that I truly knew what the risk was. Mostly, I felt content living my life and doing meaningful work. I showed up for Xandra when she went through her own struggles. So many weekends, we watched Star Trek and laughed about who we were crushing on most in each episode.

"I think Nurse Chapel in goggles is my sexuality," she said.

"Ooh, me too! Or maybe its Spock in a hoodie," I said.

We laughed, often sharing a pizza together, and enjoying dreaming of other worlds and other ways of living.

Years later, on a winter morning of bright, cold sunlight—it often seemed that the brightest days were the coldest, somehow—I was making my morning coffee when I felt so much gratitude. I had found the gentle comfort of routine again. And I was grateful for the sun rising in the morning and setting in the evening. I was so happy to be able to wake up, make breakfast, and do some work from home.

Opening my laptop, I sipped at my coffee as I checked my email. Amid the emails from other faculty, and correspondence about department meetings and end of the year exhibitions, my eyes locked on the subject line, "desde luz." I clicked on it, and inside was only a link:

https://pastebin.com/s4fkqucb

I opened it, and read the note before me with fast intensity:

Mom?

It's Luz. But these days people call me Os, for Oscuro. I think we found you. Estoy con Cora. We're in DF. It's a long story, but can you come meet us here? I didn't want to include it in this email, in case your email is being surveilled. If you get this, and I hope you do, I can't believe we got this far in trying to find you. I didn't think it would be possible. If you can, please reply tos4fkqucb@hushmail.com.

with love across universes,
Os

I sat typing at my laptop outside a stylish café in the Condesa neighborhood of Distrito Federal, Mexico City, feeling the altitude's effect on my breathing. I was sipping a café con leche and writing a digital journal entry to myself. It didn't seem possible, but I had to show up out of the smallest possibility that this could all be real. I had been communicating for weeks with someone who called herself Os, who said she was my Luz, but still, I could barely believe it.

I had been focusing on building a movement for climate justice, determined to heal the environmental damage that had been caused by corporations and politicians, and partly, too, by my own actions. I was no longer trying to break the laws of physics to suit my own desires. I felt settled again, grounded, and it had been hard to receive this news—even if it was good news—that my two great loves might be alive and reachable, and now in this universe.

As I tried to process it all, to write it all out on the patio of that lovely coffee shop, all of very modern design in bright pastels with sharp lines and stark green potted ferns hanging above my head, conveyed a thoughtfully designed aesthetic. I glanced up from my screen.

There, in the dappled shade of wide green leaves under the bright afternoon sun, was my daughter Os, running toward me, wearing a black hoodie with an embroidered satin lining in the hood, and behind her, walking fast, was Cora, her long hair laying across her well-defined shoulders, her eyes bright and locked on mine. The three of us embraced, laughed, cried.

I couldn't believe it, but I looked into Os's eyes and saw that she was not glitching at all. She was here, and she was real. I felt deep inside of myself that I would do everything I could to make sure we would remain together, as a family.

EPILOGUE:
Realida, the Network of Intergalactic Realms of Probability

One hundred years later

Looking out over the expanse of valley between the two mountains, the poet marveled at the millions of shards of light that refracted in the air above the waterfall that emitted from the northernmost peak. The mist floated up and around the finely gilded bridge that appeared to stop short in the empty air between the peaks.

She could just make out the line where the floating water particles and the bridge seemed to end but where, in fact, they entered a portal to another planet in another galaxy. Morelia captured a brief clip of it for the moving image record she was assembling of this day of celebration across the Realida, the Network of Intergalactic Realms of Probability.

Few remembered the precise details of why this day was celebrated across the realms, although all schoolchildren knew the name and face of Realidad, the scientist whose achievements a hundred years earlier had led to the advancements that were the foundations of their society.

Morelia skimmed through the archival records she'd retrieved to inform her narrative of this day's history. With her magnification on, Morelia could see the children in their best clothes raucously playing on the bridge as they waited for the pomp of the parade to start, laughing and chasing each other amid the spray. Living in the plenitude created by intergalactic probability jumps, these children had never seen events like the historic images Morelia had lately been reviewing of cities burning at night, of police shootings of young Black girls, or of the hateful face of that autocrat who took power despite losing the popular vote on this day a hundred years prior. Morelia winced at the violence of the video of a Black man murdered in his car by police that had been filmed by his girlfriend, relieved that the children playing outside would never experience these violent expressions of hatred.

One of the children on the bridge, a Black girl around ten years of age with glowing strands of color weaved into her shining locks, was being lovingly encouraged by her teacher to come join the celebration dance that was part of the parade. No, she had never seen such footage, nor did she know what the word *police* meant. The girl would be familiar with the community mediators, but her understanding of violence was far less intense than the brutality of the twenty-first century.

Morelia gazed out of the glass hemisphere that comprised her writing room, more than a hundred stories up. She had noted that in these old records, what was now simply considered vision was always described as enhanced sight, achieved through the use of prosthetic, augmented reality lenses implanted in the eyes. This was what Realidad's partner had used at a protest against the election to record police violence.

Morelia forwarded through the records of the next few months of Realidad's life in her personal archives. In an earlier age, these would have been referred to as "social media," but Morelia knew it simply as memory sharing. As a weaver of narratives, she saw no need to make distinctions between augmented technologies of memory and her brain's limited storage. She herself kept external memories in the indoor garden of her home. These were stored in memory circuits grown into the walled cells of the plants she lovingly tended, which she could access via a link with her own vision through a genetically matched graft. This, she supposed, could be described as "augmented," using the language of that era.

Yet by reviewing the archaic storage mediums of two-dimensional recordings, the old photo and video evidence, she saw how limited the technologies available in Realidad's time were. Then, too, Earth was thought of as the only planet humans could live on; their scientists had mistakenly believed that time was a limitation. Before Realidad, the simple scientific worldview conceived of time as akin to their widespread prison system—another gladly forgotten artifact of that archaic world: a network of stone buildings containing metal cages for keeping humans in. Inescapable, horrific, and inhumane.

Morelia paused the video she'd been watching—Realidad and Cora working on visual models of particle probability inside a small apartment—to breathe deeply. She sighed and placed her hand on her chest, feeling a moment of empathy for the terrifying world Realidad lived in, where hateful police put human beings into cages and where their entire, limited understanding of the universe mirrored those cages.

Feeling profound gratitude for the freedom she now experienced, Morelia looked back out at the bridge and up to the arcs of white clouds across the blushing sky. She felt so much love and appreciation for the scientists of Realidad's time who were brave enough to pose the many worlds interpretation, and advance the loop quantum gravity theory. They were the ones to reveal that time was not an inexorable forced march, but an infinite multiplicity of quanta, mirroring the infinite multiplicity of universes.

Morelia felt immense admiration, too, for the ways the science had unfolded as a dialogue. The breakthrough Realidad and Cora had made—out of their own desire to create a family—was then transformed into the technology for crossing realities by their daughter Os. Later, other scientists built on that to build devices for spanning distances that had previously been impossible. The practice of identifying moments where universes split off and then traversing those boundaries came to be called probability jumping. Realidad's use of her own theoretical proof was limited; she had only traveled within the possibilities of her own lifestream, her own personal timeline. Yet her work enabled decades of research by others who understood that if one can jump between universes, much as in the older concept of wormholes, one can cross probability holes.

The technique of probability jumping can be imagined as crossing between two spheres or bubbles, each one containing a universe. Through the creation of massive accelerators the size of cities and with proper manipulation of the velocity and torque of particles as they entered the probability hole, it was discovered that one could choose to arrive at a different location in space but the same location in time. In other words, one could "spin the bubble" of the universe one arrived in. The loop quantum gravity theory demonstrated that space and time were not contiguous, but were, in fact, made up of infinitesimally small quanta.

Then, the jump technique between the many worlds that Realidad had revealed combined with this new understanding of time and space, and human movement was no longer limited. This development came as the last of the Arctic melted, and much of the surviving human population was undertaking massive climate migration. Amid war and conflict, the step into an infinite number of other worlds was a divine kindness. The social foundations that had been built over centuries to accommodate, promote, and preserve the scarcity of capitalism on Earth quickly unraveled, as humanity drew on an absolute abundance of time and space to breathe, and reimagine itself.

Morelia could not even count the number of diplomatic debates that still raged between planets over coveted locations and new technologies. But she could at least feel immense gratitude on this day celebrating the woman who had made a new, intergalactic network of societies possible. Realidad led the way to an age of prosperity and healing none could have foreseen on that dark night one hundred years earlier.

What Morelia did not see, from her perch high up to capture the grandeur of the day, was a figure blending into the crowd of thousands of celebrants. She couldn't imagine that despite the end of scarcity, hatred could persist. Indeed, it was hard for many to conceive that bigotry could still be harbored in the hearts of some in this place full of joy and comfort, but bigotry has never made sense. The figure in the crowd carried a device in his satchel, one that might look to most people there like a sculpture, a series of curved copper pipes and a small container of fluid, some silvery particles spinning in the fluid.

Today was the day to find out. Would the machine stop a heart? Would it cause simple combustion? Or perhaps something even larger, an explosion? Amid the loud music and celebration, no one paid much attention to this person dressed in unremarkable clothing as he pressed the power button, as the liquid in his device lit up and began to spin wildly inside its container. Aiming his device toward someone in the crowd, the one who'd brought it here simply expected it might kill them. Yet in an instant, a ripple seemed to fold the air and expanded out through the crowd with a barely perceptible whine, and then everyone, including the wielder of the weapon, was gone.

Morelia gasped and dropped her recording device. Screaming, she ran down the hall to her friend's quarters, hoping she was there. Ana sat reading calmly, and she was shocked to see Morelia in her wild fit. Morelia spat out her question, asking if Ana had also seen the sudden violent event unfold. But Ana didn't know of any celebrations planned for that day in their city and hadn't seen anything unusual.

Morelia ran down the hall toward the communications office of her university—she had to get word out across the necklace of inhabited planets. The probability war had begun.

Acknowledgments

This book is the outcome of an uncountable number of particle tracks, collisions, and reactions. So many interactions between so many people, and so much love, across universes.

This book is for May. Being one of your mothers was the greatest thing that ever happened to me. You gave me a sense of purpose and a depth of love I had never known. I write this in the hopes of you having a livable life, a wonderful life, filled with love. To May's family, I could never thank you enough for welcoming me into your home. I never imagined how lucky I would be.

I want to thank all the trans femmes who showed me how to survive: this book is for you. When I started writing this, I could have never imagined how much we would be under threat, never imagined a year with almost 400 anti-trans laws proposed in the US within three months, never imagined the rapid metastasis fascism would have in the US. To all of the trans people who have transitioned into another plane of existence too soon at the hands of murderous violence, we will never forget you, and we will never stop fighting for a world where no one is murdered because of their gender.

Imagining our future, a future of love and family, feels more important than ever. Thank you, Gavilán Rayna Russom, for being such a profound friend, inspiration, and guide. I certainly wouldn't be here without you. Thank you for showing me that life is possible, Ravyn Wngz, Kiyomi Fujikawa, Trish Salah, Susan Stryker, Kai Cheng Thom, Giuseppe Campuzano, Mattie Brice, Eva Hayward, Jules Gill-Peterson, Luna Merbruja, Edxie Betts, Sasha Costanza-Chock, Lavelle Ridley, Ryka Aoki, CeCe Mcdonald, and Dani Wright. Thank you, Kate Bornstein, for writing the words, "You can do it," and setting me on a path of freedom.

I'm so grateful to Rox Samer, my queer sibling, for always inspiring me and making me laugh. Thank you for constantly reminding me of the power of science fiction.

To Ryan-Li Dahlstrom, my queer sibling, thank you for being on the path with me, for your endless care, kindness, love, and support.

To Marcia Ochoa, thank you for being my queer family, and for loving May so, so deeply and joyfully. Thank you, Jenny Kelly, Marisol Lebrón, and Isla, for all of your love, and laughs, and showing me how full of love life can be. Thank you, Michael Chemers, Farhana Basha, and Zain, for welcoming me into incredible adventures and giving me so much love and support. Thank you to Amanda Smith, Grant Whipple, and Thalo and Liana, for sharing your joy and your endless green worlds with me. Thank you, Lori Matsumoto, for being such an amazing friend. Thank you, Camilla Hawthorne, for loving May.

To adrienne maree brown, I am so inspired by you and have been since we met in Detroit so many years ago. I am so grateful to you for seeing my idea, and saying yes. This is a dream come true, and it is thanks to you. Your approach to science fiction led me to write my own. Thank you.

To adrienne and Walidah Imarisha and all the authors of *Octavia's Brood*, thank you. That book was the biggest direct inspiration for this book. Reading it, seeing you all perform it, inspired me to write science fiction.

To my brother Gabe, thank you for being there always. Thank you for taking me to comic shops and bringing video games to me when no one else was paying attention to my dreams and desires. I love you. To my sister Amy, thank you for caring for me when I needed a home.

To Jackie An, you saved my life many times. When I was writing the early drafts of this book, you shared your experience with me, with love. I am endlessly grateful to you for your friendship.

Thank you, Jill Petty, for being an amazing interlocutor, reader, and editor. Thank you, Angelica Sgouros, for your eye for detail and language! Thank you, AK Press! I have been inspired by and shaped by your books for decades. It is an absolute dream come true to have my book published with you!

To Octavia Butler, thank you for imagining worlds where Black, trans and nonbinary people, and women could survive and build new worlds. I am forever inspired by you. To Ursula K. Le Guin, thank you for giving us a bag full of stars and seeds as our model for writing new universes into being. Meeting you, and hearing about how you wrote novels while mothering, inspired me to write. To N. K. Jemisin, Nnedi Okorafor, Tamsyn Muir, Alexis Pauline Gumbs, Nisi Shawl, Amal El-Mohtar, and Max Gladstone, your sci-fi worlds filled with Black people, trans people, queer people, and lesbians brought me so much expansion, joy, and inspiration. Thank you.